Edward Turner

The Intriguers

Vol. 3

Edward Turner

The Intriguers
Vol. 3

ISBN/EAN: 9783337347437

Printed in Europe, USA, Canada, Australia, Japan

Cover: Foto ©Andreas Hilbeck / pixelio.de

More available books at **www.hansebooks.com**

THE INTRIGUERS:

OR,

PEVENSEL.

A ROMANCE OF THE BARONS' WAR.

IN THREE VOLUMES.

BY

EDWARD TURNER.

VOL. III.

LONDON :

T. CAUTLEY NEWBY, PUBLISHER,

30, WELBECK STREET, CAVENDISH SQUARE.

1873.

THE INTRIGUERS:

OR,

PEVENSEL.

———

CHAPTER I.

"What have I done to thee, my people? Stern
Are all thy dealings, but in this they pass
The limits of men's common malice."
BYRON'S *Prophecy of Dante.*

CONSIDERING the caution required to traverse a rugged and stony path almost swept by the drooping boughs of overhanging foliage, Conisburgh and Margot arrived at the junction of the

four roads with considerable celerity. For better
security against surprise the horses were fastened
to a tree shortly before the appointed rendezvous
was reached; and while Margot departed on foot
to execute her strange commission the young
servant kept watch at the four ways, the vista
which that open spot afforded in several directions offering a safeguard from any sudden attack
by hostile stragglers.

The light wind which had prevailed through-
out the day was effectually intercepted by a
dense wood. The stately oaks, mingled with the
ash, rose towards the west in regular gradations.
Scarcely a bough moved. There was not a sound
to break the stillness of nature. An impressive
quietude, almost appalling in its solemnity, conferred upon the ear a power to detect the approach
of any unwelcome intruder whom the organs of
vision might fail to observe.

What is that shrill cry! The young servant

starts frantically with wonder and alarm. Then he strode cautiously a short distance along the path from whence the sound proceeded. It is repeated somewhat louder and more thrilling. A female voice utters moans of agony and despair. The danger was great, but a man of Conisburgh's adventurous gallantry could not allow this mystery to haunt his mind without some effort at investigation. The cries were repeated again almost without intermission; yet no living object is visible.

After remaining some time in a pensive attitude, though the mysterious cries had ceased, Conisburgh deemed it advisable to return to the horses and assure himself of their safety; and in order to avoid the angle he must have described by re-traversing the main roads, he entered a narrow byway, which he imagined would lead directly to the desired spot. In this he was disappointed; the path diverged con-

siderably to the right. He was on the point of
retracing his steps when a female figure, kneeling
upon the ground, suddenly arrested his attention.
Her arms were folded upon an upright stone fixed
in the ground, and her head reclined on the elbow
joint and was turned away from the young wanderer's gaze. It was Una.

Shortly after her marriage to Robert Morton,
who declined to carry the despatch to Pevensel
on his wedding day, the unhappy damsel received
intelligence of her father's sudden death (the
jolly old landlord of the "Crown Inn"). She
was with her husband endeavouring to reach the
Prince's camp. The tears shed for her lost
parent were yet moist when her protector was
pounced upon by an advance guard of the forces
marching from Sussex. He was at once recognised as a deserter, and sentenced to death.
The wretched girl had bid him a last farewell,
and, friendless on earth, she retired to that

secluded spot where Conisburgh first made her acquaintance, there seeking that peace from heaven which the world could no longer give.

Whatever might be its cause, it was clear to Conisburgh that the prostrate stranger was in the deepest distress. He stood like a martyr bound to the stake, hesitating whether to make some ejaculation that would awaken a sense of his presence. Then step by step he gradually neared the bewildered girl, who, darting to her feet with a shout of alarm, glided back to a massive oak, and in dread of some immediate violence she extended her hand to forbid the young man's advance, while with words of kindness he essayed to soothe her fears.

" Fear me not," said Conisburgh. " By the faith all Christians hold dear I will approach no nearer. Do not waste time in useless terror. Speak at once the cause of this excessive grief, perchance I may prove a welcome friend."

" What have I done to merit these cruel dealings?" replied Una, picturing Conisburgh as a
deceiver who had followed her from the camp at
Kenilworth. " Your base design against a
friendless girl surpasses the limit of man's per-
secutions. It is the act of a demon! I say
begone! How shall I trust one whose comrades
murder my unhappy husband?"

" You mistake me," returned Conisburgh ; " I
am in the Prince's service, and if your husband
has suffered any wrong from my master's enemies,
I offer a friendly protection. Is it Una that I
am addressing?"

"Think not to entrap me with such false-
hoods," replied Una. " You are a vile and base
deceiver. How could my name be so familiar to
a stranger in the Prince's service? I trust you
not, and heaven will frustrate the evil that
possesses your loathsome heart."

" I do implore you to be reasonable," answered

Conisburgh. "My heart is utterly innocent of any evil designs. I am here to rescue your husband, and he shall embrace you once more in two hours."

"It will not further your purpose to mock my bitter grief," replied Una. "I will trust no man in these times of horror. You dare to follow me with thoughts of the blackest evil, and then presume to ask my confidence."

"I am most seriously misjudged, though it is beyond the power of my tongue to convince you," said Conisburgh. "I will retire or remain at your bidding; but let me beg of you to remain at this spot for two hours. If I do not then return with your husband, believe me no more. I have made a serious effort for his escape, and with Heaven's help it may succeed."

"Will I remain until you concert measures to remove me by force? No," answered Una. "Your pretended effort to relieve my lost husband is a contemptible invention. Go, you sinful and degenerate wretch, and delay not the repentance of your wickedness!"

"I will bind myself by any sacred oath you may desire; more I cannot do," answered Conisburgh, "could you but believe I am no monster of iniquity. My words are simple truth. Here have I come to sympathise with your sorrow, to protect you—nay, more—to convey an assurance that the impending calamity may yet be averted."

If due allowance is made for the depravity of the times, it is no matter of surprise that, after enduring the grossest insults for several days from her husband's captors, Una should be reluctant to place confidence in a stranger, who accosted her under such peculiar circumstances. She remained silent and contemplative for several moments; then, placing one hand on her forehead, while the other, which had been extended towards the misguided youth, dropped to her side, she uttered a cry of misery that pierced Conisburgh's sensitive heart. He darted forward impulsively, when, struck with a sudden return of terror, the terrified girl vanished behind the oak tree into a dense thicket, at once escaping from sight. The young man rushed forward and implored the girl to return, and for once to believe that there are some on earth capable of being influenced by worthy motives. His voice only produced a louder and more rapid rustling in the short brushwood, which gradually waxed fainter and fainter until inaudible in the distance. To pursue was hopeless, so he returned by the way that he came, and stands caressing the halting steeds.

It was some three hours before Conisburgh espied the peddler running towards him with breathless haste. As may easily be imagined, the story of Una's distrust awakened the deepest interest to the anxious fugitive. Guided by his new friend, he entered the thicket at the same opening where his frightened wife had disappeared. He calls as loudly as a pair of exhausted lungs can bawl. There is no response. But remembering that Una had left him with the determination of proceeding to Worcester, where some distant relation of her late father's once flourished as a wealthy citizen, the husband firmly believed they might meet again in this life. So mounting one of the steeds, while Conisburgh, on the other, indicated the road, the two adventurers arrived at the Prince's Camp, and are received by Sandford with due congratulations.

" What service do you propose to render us for this succour from the malice of old friends?" said Sandford, " wherein did you give them offence? it will be a point of charity to teach you who is the best master."

" First let my thanks be spoken to whomsoever

they may be due," replied Morton; "neither is it for me to select the fashion of my service. I await your honourable commands, and must obey in all humility."

"If able to keep a secret, and to act promptly on emergencies, you will not find us hard task-masters," returned Sandford. "Are you pre-pared to remain with us for good or evil?"

"I have no choice in the matter," answered Morton. "My old comrades seek to take my life. I refused to carry a scroll to Pevensel, and swore to enter the Prince's service; hence my offence. On the road to this camp I became a prisoner, and, save for your honourable assist-ance, a halter would have pressed my neck. You can be sure, then, it is impossible I can betray you. I am ready and willing to swear allegiance, and to undertake any post, however perilous."

"You will soon be valuable, if able to give

true answers to plain questions," returned Sandford. " How did you manage to pass out of the
camp?"

" Without a single challenge," said Morton.
" The slaves are so debauched, that they can
hardly distinguish between friend or foe. I will
wager there are not three hundred sober men
amongst them."

" Let the hounds eat, drink, and be merry for
the last time," replied Sandford. " If my words
will avail anything, we are upon them at sunrise
to-morrow."

" Place me in the van," returned Morton,
" and I will point out the tent of every lordly
rebel. At daybreak it is their custom to bathe in
a small stream, at least those who have recovered
from the last night's revelry."

" I am glad to find you so apt," replied Sandford. " It is not in my power to promise rewards,
but I will conduct you to the presence of another

who no doubt will confer a post worthy of acceptance."

The allotted six hours had nearly passed away, when Sandford and the released captive stood before the scion of Royalty, who was determined to strike some decisive blow to retrieve the fortunes of his father, still a prisoner with the Earl of Leicester. Anxious to learn the result of these deliberations, De Meudon followed, his agitated manner being calculated to attract attention, if not even to excite sympathy from all who beheld it. The favours shewn to his rival by the Prince impressed the young Knight with a belief that Sandford's hopes were not such mad conceptions as hitherto supposed. A sense of internal mortification seized the rejected lover's soul, and he longed for an advance to Kenilworth that might afford him an opportunity of crushing his opponent's prospects, and prepare the way to claim the fulfilment of Savoy's promise.

The course of operations seemed so palpable as to need little further consideration. In the black gloom of midnight the troops grope their way through the forest, aided by the lurid glare of a few torches. Conisburgh and Morton, being familiar with the road, led the van, each carrying a light. Suddenly two female figures were seen to approach, the one an old woman with dishevelled hair, who it is easy to recognise as Margot; the other, much younger in years, followed timidly, still afraid to face the marching troopers. Morton's eyes were completely dazzled by the flambeau which he held. It rendered the surrounding objects more opaque by contrast. He was scarcely aware that anyone was near, except his companions in arms, until Una rushed forward and clasped him round the neck, trembling with emotion from head to foot. Anxious to discharge his new duties, the young husband tenderly reassured the frantic girl as

soon as possible, and desiring her to follow with
Margot in the rear, he steadily leads the way. It
is solemn and dark. As they near the enemy's
camp, all torches are ordered to be extinguished.
The measured tread of soldiery sounds through
the silent groves. It is a knell that summons
some brave spirits home.

CHAPTER II.

" He was a youth of bold renown,
    Such prowess none could check,
Until by cruel foes struck down
    His frame there lay a wreck.
His courage bold inspired from birth,
    Its thrills are felt no more;
A loss that many friends on earth
    With sorrow all deplore."

ANONYMOUS.

NOT only in historical record has the Castle of Kenilworth been rendered famous to all futurity, but its former magnificence has been the principal scene of one of the finest romances that ever issued from the pen of man. Those who would

desire a fascinating description of this princely
domain cannot do better than refer to the twenty-
fifth chapter of Sir Walter Scott's novel of
" Kenilworth," where the beauties of this once
grand structure are painted with those powers of
descriptive colouring which that inimitable author
has alone been capable of exercising. For the
present it may suffice to say that it is well known
as one of the grandest relics of antiquity in England; it covers nearly the same space of ground
as old Pevensey, and, if more defined in archi-
tectural beauty, it would probably yield on the
score of antiquity; and though its origin has
been ascribed to a Saxon king of Mercia, it is
more probable that its foundation would date to
an early period after the Norman conquest.

It was on the second day of a memorable month
of August that the sun had just risen on this
noted spot, when the Royal forces advanced
rapidly to the camp that extended beneath the

walls of the venerable Castle,—at this time the great stronghold of the usurping barons. No hoarse winded bugle heralded their approach—no wild cries for bloodthirsty revenge warned the unprepared foe, who, with few exceptions, became prisoners before they had time to resist, several who were bathing, including Simon de Mountfort the younger, escaping into the Castle in a state of complete nudity. Thus was this powerful force that lately threatened Pevensel with destruction crushed almost without a show of resistance, and Leicester was despoiled of his principal reliance for reinforcements.

Shortly before this rush upon the hostile camp, a youthful warrior retained the services of Morton to point out the spot where De Vere's tent sheltered the dew moistened ground. A victim to contending passions, the young man advanced with a reckless impetuosity that almost marred the success resulting from the cool deliberation of

the mass of the attacking army. With the
ferocity of an infuriated animal De Meudon
attacked his wily enemy, receiving a blow inflicted by the massive strength of De Vere,
followed by several others from the surrounding
men at arms that stretched him low upon the
turf-clothed ground. At that moment he would
probably have drawn his last breath had not
Sandford pushed forward with an overwhelming
force; and while the retainers are made prisoners,
De Vere, in the general confusion, contrived to
effect an escape into the Castle, in company with
his naked comrade, when by a more judicious
course of action the Knight of Hurstingham
would doubtless have been numbered with the
captives.

The striking peculiarity of this brief contest
was the immense number of prisoners captured
with comparatively little bloodshed;—a circumstance not a little remarkable in an age when

warfare consisted mostly of desperate hand to hand encounters. But so completely was the re-posing army of De Mountfort surprised that many fell into the hands of their captors before they had leisure to arm, though it was previously ascertained that numbers were gorged with drink. These slept on, unconscious of their impending fate.

After the commotion excited by this sudden *ruse de guerre* had subsided, a small group as-sembled in the tent lately occupied by Rochfort de Vere, where the battered form of De Meudon had been removed. The expiring Knight lay pros-trate on the ground, his head being gently sup-ported by the arm of the thoughtful Una, while she alternately administered stimulants and bathed his temples with cool and refreshing waters obtained from the neighbouring stream. Morton and Conisburgh stood near, handing the potent liquid, or the bowl of water, as required.

Opposite to them Sandford knelt upon the ground, and placed his ear close to the mouth of the youthful sufferer, in order to catch the faint words he was endeavouring to utter. Several men at arms made up a background to the impressive scene, standing in line at a respectful distance. In this interval Margot occupied herself by placing all the various packages the fugitive had left behind in convenient order, that Sandford might examine them when able to find leisure for the undertaking.

"Unbuckle my jerkin, and you will find a small token, given me by the Lady Emmeline de Savoy in early childhood," said De Meudon, in broken whispers. "Tell her how I have treasured it, and in receiving it back, ask her to value it, as conveying the last blessings of a sincere friend."

"Your desires shall be faithfully fulfilled," replied Sandford. "Believe my intentions honest,

and confide any other matters that may concern
you on earth. Then make your peace with
heaven."

"I commend the fair lady to your care," answered De Meudon; "but there is something
more. The inheritance of my fathers was
attainted to enrich that vile knight whose banner
pollutes the walls of Hurstingham. Hunt him
to death; and let all witness my last will. If
those domains should be restored to their lawful
possessors, my name being extinct, I would have
them conferred on the one who now presses my
hand."

"Say, then, that any angry words between us
are forgiven," said Sandford.

"Truly forgiven in the sight of heaven," said
the dying knight. "Let me die as a Christian,
for as such I have endeavoured to live; and
listen—"

The syllables which followed waxed fainter and

fainter, and failed to make themselves audible even with the closest attention. A cumbered breath is snatched convulsively at long and irregular intervals. The glaring sun broke through a crevice in the tent. It falls upon the ghastly countenance of one to whom all is darkness. Those gay humours that excited merriment at many a kingly feast are silent for ever; the spirit is gone, and the bloom of youth lies broken like a withered flower. No sorrow can restore what is lost; so peace be unto his soul, we must pursue the fortunes of the living.

Hardly had the young knight drawn his last breath, before the old father confessor entered the tent. He had been summoned immediately after the fight, but either he slept with the others who were overpowered by good cheer, or some more profitable exercise of his holy office had occupied the time. If an impartial observer could judge by his chagrin when he found that all was too late, it is probable he was not aware of priestly unctions being required by a dying baron, or the happy dead might not have departed without the benefit of absolution, and mother church might have been the richer for the old father's quickened zeal.

" Peace be to all," said the priest; "this is what heaven has wrought by its chosen instrument; any poor service I might have rendered is needless. Yet where is the provision for the religious rites requisite for the repose of his soul?"

" Silence, thou churlish priest," replied Sandford; "seek not to make terms with one who requires nothing but Christian burial. Whatever may be needful to inter his bones as becomes a worthy knight is thine, and something further to buy thy good will."

" Nay, but what gifts hath the good man proffered to redeem his soul from the company of men of Belial," returned the priest. "These heresies will provoke the wrath of heaven. A godless man, who has neither done penance nor received absolution, claims the prayers of our holy church without fee or offering."

"It is no fault of mine, my holy father was too late for the exaction of any gift from the dying sinner," retorted Sandford; "but there is no doubt a wealthy spoil in this tent that will compensate for the rites of burial, and satisfy your holy conscience for the absence of penance and absolution."

"So far then I may perhaps yield without incurring the holy father's displeasure," said the priest, in drawling tones. "Though no masses can be solemnised for a child of earth who has departed into purgatory without the blessing of our church."

"I would rather bargain with a Jew for his shekels, than with a priest for his benedictions," replied Sandford. "I cannot put words in a dead man's mouth, even to confer treasure on the church. Take what I have to offer, or perchance such obstinacy may prove your greater loss."

"The protection of Our Lady be upon you," said the priest, afraid to provoke a disagreement, lest Sandford should recant his proposals. "My good service is at your command; and may the sins of our departed friend lay lightly on him. If it so pleases you the body can be removed to the Priory of St. Nicholas. There, under the shady willow, shall his bones rest in that long sleep, which the clarions of omnipotence can alone arouse."

"Thanks, worthy priest," returned Sandford, "I am ignorant of what treasure those chests may contain; if much, it will better requite your service, but if little, you must accept it as all my power can bestow."

The remains of the deceased knight are placed

on a litter, and, supported by men at arms, move forward towards their last resting-place. The old priest led the way, Conisburgh, Morton, and his little wife following the mournful procession. While they were thus occupied, Sandford, assisted by Margot, opened the chests, and as De Vere had received no benefit from the sacking of Winchester, the amount of treasure was miserably deficient. When the holy father returned, he received his quota in silence, though he did not fail to indicate the depth of his disappointment, by a significant curl of the lip.

The conclusion of this business enabled Sandford to peruse in quietude the various documents left by De Vere on his sudden flight. The first scroll that met the young man's eye offered large rewards for his capture, whether dead or alive. By its mauled and dirty condition it had evidently been extensively exhibited amongst his enemies. This he consigned to destruction by tearing it

in fragments. Then several worthless papers
shared a similar fate. The next of any importance was the confiscation of the domain at
Hurstingham, and its gift to Rochfort de Vere.
Of this our hero took possession. There was but
one more of any consequence, the attainder on
Savoy's estates in Sussex, this also was retained
to be cancelled, when the King's authority was
fully restored.

The necessity for some immediate action, to
follow up the success he had so far attained,
smothered in the exigency of the moment that sincere grief which Sandford could not suppress at the
untimely end of his powerful rival. A communication from the Prince requested his views
concerning the next proceeding, and as a preli-
minary step, it was determined to withdraw to
the hill, from whence the army started on the
previous night. But two hours were allowed
to refresh the troops, and with that unceasing

energy that marked all his actions at this turning point of his life, Sandford made use of this interval to good account, while most of the army pledged the Prince's health in bumpers of good wine taken from the enemy. He is still in De Vere's tent in company with the faithful Conisburgh, Morton, Una, and Margot.

"My good friends," said Sandford, "it is useless to trifle with nature, let us refresh ourselves in moderation with the good cheer left by our foes, unless the holy fathers of St. Nicholas have taken care of you already."

"I never broke fast at a priest's expense yet," replied Conisburgh; "the holy men are generally receivers, not givers of good things. Having loaded their own table, they content themselves by remembering all fellow Christians in their prayers. I have not tasted sup or bit since last sunset."

"Then help yourselves as inclination may

prompt," replied Sandford; "these are not times for ceremony. First, in solemn silence, we will drink to the memory of our lost companion. May heaven give him peace above !"

" I wish him happiness hereafter to all eternity," returned Conisburgh, " though I would rather he had been a little more cool and let us have captured that brute at whose orders my back has borne many a blow."

" Waste no time in regrets," answered Sandford; "his game is nearly played out, and with good judgment we shall catch him yet."

" And woe be to his skin if he falls into my power," replied Conisburgh. " I have seen many a good man hacked to pieces inch by inch before his sight; it would chill the strongest blood to hear half his cruelties."

" I doubt it not," said Sandford; " but too eager a thirst for revenge may defeat its own

object. This you have just witnessed in the fate
of that young Knight. If I entrust you
with an onerous duty, will you be calm and
thoughtful?"

" You may trust me," replied Conisburgh.

" Then," continued Sandford, " it is my purpose to leave you in a neighbouring wood with
six score men; about thirty of them will be
mounted. Margot will keep watch round the
Castle. Should that worthy Knight of Hurstingham leave the protection of its walls retain him
as a prisoner if possible; but dead or alive he
must be secured. The prize is worth the venture,
but it will need all the patience human nature is
capable of exercising. Above all things never
venture to show yourselves out of cover, or some
counter snare may entrap you, and bring destruction on your own heads. I must proceed with
the Prince to attack Leicester in his own
stronghold, and Morton, being well acquainted

with his late master's habits, will accompany
me."

Morton simply bowed an acquiescence, while
Conisburgh repeated an assurance that he might
be trusted to undertake the proposed enterprise.
The men for this service were told off, and Sandford proceeded to place them at a suitable ambush,
and there bade them farewell, with many wishes
for success. He told them they must not anticipate that De Vere would venture to leave the
Castle for some days; and if attacked by too
heavy a force they could make a retreat by a road
he took the precaution to indicate. This done he
returned to the scene of his late exploits, and
found Morton and his good little spouse quite
prepared to follow him, wherever fate might
direct the way.

There is generally some marked period in most
men's lives when the tide of fortune turns either
for good or evil; and though many may drag

through an existence without any favourable op-
portunities, numbers have let them pass, wanting
the confidence to avail themselves of the proffered
advantages.   At this moment Sandford's career
seemed to have risen within one or two steps of
its summit.   He was aware of it; nor did he fail
to remember that many have attained a similar
point, only to fall more rapidly than they
ascended, owing to some unhappy error of judgment.   Under these impressions he did not relax
in his circumspection.   But the scene before us
is too busy and exciting for these reflections.
The victorious army is retracing its march, not in
the dreariness of night, not in that silent antici-
pation of some coming event longed for with inward eagerness, the dense forest, instead of
deepening the dim shades of early dawn, afforded
a welcome shade from the blazing sun; while
shouts of triumph are mingled with martial
music, brayed out by the rudest instruments. So

the time passes merrily away until the troopers are drawn up on the same ground from whence they started in doubt and uncertainty, and with appetites sharpened by exertion they discuss their evening meal.

CHAPTER III.

"Nay, be thou sure, I will requite thy kindness,
For that it made my imprisonment a pleasure;
Aye, such pleasure as encaged birds
Conceive, when, after many moody thoughts,
At last, by notes of household harmony,
They quite forget their loss of liberty."

3rd Part King Henry VI.

WHEN the powers of an energetic man are put severely to the test, the conceptions of his brain will often follow on the emergency with a truly astounding rapidity. No sooner was it announced to Sandford that the Prince had received information of Leicester's sojourn near Worcester,

than doubt and uncertainty perplexed the young
man's mind. He believed it only some treacher-
ous reports emanating from the Earl's spies, who
were desirous to draw the Prince away, while a
junction was effected with the reinforcements at
Kenilworth, of whose destruction they were no
doubt in ignorance.

There is always a suspicion and rancour entertained towards men who can boast greater wisdom
than their neighbours. Instead of his success
gaining the confidence of those with whom he
was associated in the Prince's councils, Sandford
found any further proposal he might venture to
offer most vigorously opposed. But with the
calmness of a reasonable man he kept his mouth
shut and his ears open, and determined to take
upon himself the responsibility of any course of
action which he individually should deem it ex-
pedient to pursue. This prejudice might be
jealousy resulting from ignorance. Every at-

tempt to soften the hostility by condescension was worse than useless. The more he endeavoured to make allowance for his opponents' folly and weakness, the more the opposition brought against him increased in proportion.

On the morning following the ruse upon Kenilworth, the march to Worcester was continued in full earnest, quite against Sandford's inclinations. But he had no intention to permit his master's cause to be impaired by any error, however slight. Hastily collecting a few trustworthy followers, the young man started on a reconnoissance, determined to discover the exact position of Leicester's forces if possible. Taking a direction towards the south-west, he had only proceeded a few miles, when entering into conversation with some rustics, it was ascertained that a large force had passed the river at Kempsey, about four miles south of Worcester.

No longer had Sandford any doubt that his

conjectures were correct. The Prince was mis-
informed. But as the young wanderer stood
across the direct line of the march of the hostile
forces, it was necessary to retreat with all possible
speed. After crossing the river Avon by a rude
bridge, he halted at Offenham, keeping watch for
several hours; nor were his expectations disappointed. The cavalcades of hostile warriors approached, and, as he had supposed, took up their
quarters for the night at the neighbouring town
of Evesham.

But greater fortune was yet to result from the
young adventurer's expedition. On venturing to
the brink of the river Avon to refresh his horse
from its clear waters, he was accosted by a
trooper who had pushed forward to the opposite
bank with a similar intention. To Sandford's
utter surprise, he was recognised as an old acquaintance by one that formerly took an active
part with the Prince, but who latterly had re-

mained with the King during a protracted
captivity, and who was still in attendance upon
his sovereign. This courtier, by name Ralph de
Ardernne, made a signal for Sandford to retire,
while he galloped round the old bridge. Thus
he crossed the river, and the two horsemen stand
alone, their right hands entwined in the grasp of
friendship.

"What is more cheering than the face of an
old friend?" said De Ardernne. "I believed you
a banished wanderer, no longer engaged in
knight errant adventures on the shores of Old
England."

"Such was the determination of my enemies,"
replied Sandford. "But without being rash, I
have no notion of playing the craven before an
usurping lord. How fares my good lord the
King?"

"My liege is well and hearty," replied De
Ardernne, "and during a sojourn with the

fathers of Evesham, his stomach will suffer
nothing but a loss of appetite. What is your
purpose in wandering here ?"

"Not to play the truant," said Sandford.
" My royal liege has surprised the army at
Kenilworth. Not a man remains free to tell the
tale, except a few that are caged within the
Castle's walls. I watch for Leicester's advance,
that some blow may follow to release the King."

" It is well," said De Ardernne. "You may
rely on my secresy, for I am weary of this
restraint. Go, return to your master; tell him
Leicester rests here to-night, and in my judgment to-morrow's vesper bell will sound before
he departs. I remain with the King, who in the
skirmish will need some trusty friend."

" Be that so," replied Sandford; " keep your
own counsel, even before the King himself. Let
nothing be suspected. I will wager my life the
Prince's army is here by daybreak."

" Let us be quick, or my very absence may betray us," said De Ardernne. " To-night will many waste their hours in sleep, and eat of food they may not live to digest. Before daybreak I will have the only bridge destroyed by which any can hope to escape. Get you gone, and may we meet again in freedom, to celebrate the brightest days of our existence."

The informer soon disappeared, recrossing the old bridge that was doomed to destruction in a few hours. Sandford was not slow to follow his example, though in a totally opposite direction. With the hostile army before him, it was impossible to take a direct course to Worcester, so proceding northward by way of Bitford to Alcester, he then veered to the left, and almost arrived at the old city with the rear of the Prince's army. First impressions are often the truest, and our young hero was now convinced beyond the possibility of error. His conjectures formed in the

morning were unquestionably correct, but when
ushered into the Prince's presence he was so exhausted with recent exertion, that the son of
royalty insisted on his partaking of a banquet
then hastily prepared. Thus was Sandford left
alone to tell his story, untrammelled by the
jealousies of any petty opponents.

Yet the day was by no means spent. There
was time for more than a mere recapitulation of
the scenes just witnessed. The surrounding warriors would need some hours' repose, and it is
hardly possible to find a man so patriotic as to
smother every private desire that may haunt his
honest breast, even in the midst of turmoil and
war's alarms. Sandford well knew that the information he now possessed was almost invalu-
able. Leicester was halting in a locality where,
under the surprise of a sudden attack, the peculiar ·nature of the country would prevent all
possibility of escape, as will hereafter be described.

Why might not our young hero indulge hopes of advancement to result from his exertions? And what might not such advancement bring in its train? All those prejudices that pride had conceived within a venerable breast would be crushed. That rank which would flatter the vanity of a lofty soul might be attained, nor was it requisite to speak, for the royal Prince anticipated these thoughts—

" I would fain have been spared this unpleasantness," said the Prince. " But your plans not having been accepted at this morning's conference, am I to presume you withdraw from my councils? Come, account for this day of idleness, and remember that for services already rendered the very highest honours await you, when my father is released from bondage."

" May it please my royal liege," replied Sandford, " my conjectures offered this morning might have been right or wrong. If you were

pleased to deem them erroneous, far be it from
me to take offence, or to question the superi-
ority of my liege's judgment. I have been no
idler, and since I parted from you the position of
the enemy is within my certain knowledge."

"I fully believed it so," returned the Prince.
"You may be sure I will requite your energies.
I know your ambition, it is for honours that will
make Savoy proud to confer the hand of his
lovely niece upon you. In that you shall not be
disappointed, but leave me not at this critical
moment."

"Everything is secure if my liege's cause
flourishes until I desert it," answered Sandford.
"My hopes you may guess aright, nor am I
ashamed to ask a favour of my liege, though my
service shall be ever at command, if deemed
worthy of acceptance."

"Be sure that everything asked which my
power can confer is already yours," replied the

Prince. "It makes the recollection of my imprisonment a pleasure, when, in a great measure, I owe my liberty to so worthy a friend, for such I now esteem you. But, tell me how did Savoy requite you for relieving the Castle?"

"I would rather have avoided a subject so unpleasant," said Sandford. "Let it be sufficient to say I am forbidden to revisit his domain."

"He shall ask your forgiveness, or suffer for it," said the Prince. "Until he does, my father shall never re-confer upon him the estates which have been declared forfeited."

"Nay, my royal liege," replied Sandford, "remember his venerable years. Such trouble might bring those grey hairs with sorrow to an untimely end. Let us hope my liege's words might possess sufficient power to soften his animosity."

"That I have endeavoured to do already," said the Prince. "Expressly at my desire my mother has sent for the Lord of Pevensel to

Guildford; she, doubtless, may influence his mind in your favour; he may be there already."

"It is impossible," replied Sandford. "When I quitted Pevensel he could not rise from his couch. Though three whole weeks have since passed."

"Then may a sick bed give him time to think better of his discourtesy," answered the Prince. "When Leicester has fallen you shall away to Guildford with the intelligence, backed by a heavy force for my mother's better protection. I am confident we shall soon be victorious; our men must outnumber the enemy two to one."

"If my voice yet avails in your honourable councils, my Lord of Leicester is in my liege's power by to-morrow night," returned Sandford.

"In my anxiety to do you full justice, I had forgotten you were to account for this day's proceedings," said the Prince. "Say on—and never did man speak to a more willing listener."

"Then," replied Sandford, "my Lord of

Leicester is with the King at Evesham, entertained by the monks of the abbey. The bridge over the Avon will be destroyed to-night, and so all escape from any justice my liege may be pleased to inflict will be prevented."

" At Evesham !" said the Prince, much bewildered, " know you this of a certainty, or is it the deception of some worthless spy? I believe there are such amongst us."

" Undoubtedly there are, or my liege would not have been deceived this morning," returned Sandford. " If my eyesight is reliable, I have seen the forces enter Evesham from a distant mound. But more than that, I have even succeeded in obtaining an interview with my liege's faithful servant, Ralph de Ardernne."

" Your energies are inexhaustible," replied the Prince ; " there is nothing too difficult or too hazardous for your fearless nature. How long does the army rest at Evesham ?"

"Until to-morrow's vesper bell," said Sandford; "if I can further prevail upon my liege we are there by daybreak. Let the van carry the standards taken at Kenilworth, and the enemy will rush to meet us as friends, only to meet their destruction."

"By heavens!" returned the Prince, "had you been by my side at Lewes, these disasters would never have occurred. Let us pray for a fortunate issue; nor shall we leave this place without imploring the aid of Omnipotence in the cause of the right."

"Let me presume once more to offer a suggestion," said Sandford; "there are spies amongst us, my liege is already aware of it."

"It is to be deplored," answered the Prince; "but by no earthly power can we discriminate between right and wrong in such vast numbers of men. The valour displayed by our soldiers proves that the faithless are few and far between."

"If we cannot detect them," continued Sandford, "we can at least blind their eyes to our purposes until it is too late to frustrate them. Let the troops file through the old city of Worcester, and march for two or three miles in the direction of Bridgenorth, then wheeling to the right towards Alcester, we shall yet reach Evesham by daybreak."

"It is well spoken again," said the Prince; "in two hours the first detachment shall be on the march, and should our precarious travels come to a fortunate issue, what further favour can I confer? Those already promised are for past services."

"There is one I am unwilling to speak," replied Sandford, "lest my liege should not deem it asked in good faith."

"The devotion you have always shown would forbid my entertaining such an imagination," returned the Prince. "I can only repeat that everything shall be granted which my power can execute."

"Then my liege is aware that our success at Kenilworth was only marred by the loss of a young and valorous knight," said Sandford. "Zeal proved his destruction; but he has left a dying wish, though I would rather it had reached my liege's ears by other lips than mine."

"And who could have conveyed it better?" said the Prince.

"I will certainly convey it truthfully, though it may seem selfish," continued Sandford. "The domains of Hurstingham were attainted from this young knight's father, and given to Rochfort de Vere; the document is in my possession. The name of De Meudon is blotted out for ever; but by the dying words of the last bearing that honourable distinction, words spoken in the presence of many witnesses, he desired that they might be conferred upon myself."

"Consider it granted before it is asked," said the Prince. "Yet you astonish me; how did the document come into your possession."

"I found it amongst the papers left in De Vere's tent," replied Sandford. "I have also the forfeiture of Savoy's domains in Sussex. There was nothing else that concerned anyone but the owner, so I consigned them to destruction."

"It shall be done, as you desire, the moment my father is released, and given with your patent of honours," replied the Prince. "But let us rise to the duties that are now pressing. May to-morrow's sunset afford you all that is asked, and half as much as you deserve would exceed all that I could possibly give."

Flowing imperceptibly over our heads, the tide of time will often soothe calamities already

endured ; but it only increases any apprehension
of future terror that may haunt the mind; and
the further any coming events are beyond the
scope of actual knowledge, the wider the range of
fancy respecting them. Three weeks had elapsed
since Sandford quitted the walls of Pevensel. In
that short space his fortunes brightened from
day to day; but there is often danger in
prosperity, where adversity will prompt its own
safeguard, and the good offices of a friend are
not always bestowed with proper caution. The
Lady Emmeline had been summoned to leave the
Castle. After the injunctions Sandford left, she
would only do so in misery and fear, if the proposal did not produce a further estrangement
from her guardian. The Prince had been influenced by the best of motives in promoting the
consummation of a happy and lasting union; but
there were yet watchers round Pevensel. Even

if able to prevail upon his niece to make the journey to Guildford, would Savoy exercise that precaution needful in times of danger, or by some fatal oversight all might be yet lost, and the bloom of Nature's fairest flower cut off by the wintry blast of violence and oppression. To-morrow must witness a fearful struggle. The anxious youth would perhaps then be free to exercise his care over that tender maiden; but the coming battle would be one of life or death. He might not survive that scene of carnage. The night was dark and gloomy. Hot and sultry the breathless atmosphere forebodes the coming of a mighty tempest, while the warlike troopers march steadily to victory or death. The hours glide along. Grim and faint through the glimmer of breaking day, the proud towers of Evesham rise majestically in the distant view.

In the midst of this solemn march one gay and blooming face is missed ; worn down with fatigue and excitement, the careful Una is left with her relation at Worcester, who had never yet set eyes upon his kinsman's child, while Morton started on the wide world of fortune, mingling in scenes of commotion and strife.

CHAPTER IV.

"Suiche was the mothere of Eivesham,
    Vor bataile non it was."
                    ROBERT OF GLOUCESTER.

WHETHER the result of a ferocious contest, which occurred on the fourth day of August, in the year of our Lord twelve hundred and sixty-five, would mark its influence on all succeeding generations of mankind, or whether the present condition of society would have been precisely the same had this circumstance never taken place, is a meta-physical calculation not quite within the limits of this work. But there can be no doubt that the memorable battle, to which it is now requisite to make some allusion, produced in its time, and for many subsequent years, a complete revolution in the political development of this country's progress, and must also have shown a corresponding effect on those vicissitudes of domestic life which this story is an endeavour to depict.

That gentle river, which takes its source at Naseby, in Northamptonshire, after passing the town that gave birth to England's immortal bard, swells into a considerable stream, and flows on to the valley which sweeps from the base of the Cotswold Hills. Here the still gliding waters describe a semicircle in the form of a horseshoe; leaving a promontory of land, whereon the ancient town of Eovesham, or as it is more commonly termed in modern phraseology Evesham, rises in regular gradations until crowned by the ruins of that once extensive abbey, which, legend would have us believe, was erected on a piece of land begged from the King of the Mercians, by the good St. Egwin, who, after being miraculously pardoned from his sins on returning from a pilgrimage to Rome, was desirous to make some atonement for his unmitigated crime in becoming enamoured with three beautiful virgins, supernaturally produced from the litter of an old sow, lost by that unhappy swain Eoves, a worthy public guardian of the pigs of the servants of God. But it is more within the limits of probability that the good saint was charmed with the loveliness of the fertile vale, stretching in one magnificent vista to the Malvern range, and on this account selected it as a suitable spot for the erection of a temple to celebrate the great Creator's praise.

In this holy edifice rested our good King Henry the Third, still a captive to the Earl of Leicester.

The latter was desirous to push forward, and join the forces of his son, that now existed only in the imagination of his brain. But having heard of the excellent dinners with which the holy fathers at Evesham entertained their guests, his majesty had no notion of proceeding without partaking of the cheer. It is possible also that Leicester would have " Sung and laughed, and the rich wine quaffed" had the Prince been less active in his movements. Nor can it be imagined that those notables would have been disappointed at the hospitality of the holy gourmands, when early records inform us that on the feast of the Holy Trinity, and no doubt on many other grand occasions, each monk was allowed one capon and a quart of wine, the Prior being apportioned two capons and half a flagon of the same liquid, while the old Abbot himself was expected to do his duty as an Englishman by devouring no less than three capons, which were to be washed down his capacious throat with a whole flagon of the juice of the grape.

When the daylight had so far broken the darkness of night that the eye could distinguish a distant object, the van of the Prince's army approached the town in the direction of the Alcester road, carrying the standards captured at Kenilworth. This stratagem was of course more deceptive in an age, when human vision was obliged to exercise its capabilities without the aid of a telescope; but the fatal banners soon attracted the attention of a far-sighted individual, who has been described as the first known amateur in England that studied the art of heraldry. This barber, by name Nicholas, is said to have ascended the clock tower of the abbey—though it must be presumed to be the tower in which a clock was subsequently erected, unless the monks of Evesham were a few years in advance of their fellow countrymen in the study of

horological science ; from this eminence the dis-
cerning man discovered the approach of friendly
standards, though carried by hostile hands. He
was not slow to impart what he considered a piece
of joyful intelligence ; but no sooner had the Earl .
arrived to watch the supposed advance of his son,
than the same learned Theban descried the banners of the Prince, of Gloucester, and of Mortimer bringing up the rear in one dense and compact mass. The truth was soon revealed, and
Leicester perceiving the trap into which he had
fallen, gave vent to the impressive exclamation,
" May the Lord have mercy on our souls, our
bodies are the Prince's."

A touching little episode followed. Leicester's
son endeavoured to persuade his father to fly and
escape the coming ruin; but the elder warrior
was determined, and entreated his son to leave
that he might not perish in the bloom of youth.
Both remained faithful to the post of duty; and

after giving every man leave to depart who feared the issue of the contest, the Earl, invoking the protection of heaven, led forth his band to encounter the approaching hordes, before whom his little army seemed as a speck in the clouds, or as a worm that was to be crushed under the foot of a giant.

The army of the Prince was drawn up on an eminence, north of the town, called Greenhill. The forces of Leicester occupied an opposite mound, having the town at their back, the winding river skirting both their flanks. In the valley between, the scene of carnage began. The old King, placed by the Earl in the front, fell wounded in the shoulder, and would have perished on the spot, but crying out, " I am Henry of Winchester, your king," his voice reached the ear of the ever active Prince, who at once removed his father to a place of safety. So this murderous battle continued until evening. A black darkness overspread the beautiful valley. The combatants were scarcely able to distinguish between friend or foe, while the vivid lightning poured forth its liquid fire in one continuous stream, the clashing of arms being drowned in the rolling peals of solemn thunder, until the warring elements struck terror into the hearts of men, and men to whom the din of battle was but a familiar sound. This latter circumstance has been recorded on good authority, and must not be deemed a flight of imagination, designed to give colouring to the scene of strife.

The Earl himself fought with desperation. His prowess called forth a remark that eight such men might have turned the fortune of the day, but towards evening the greater number of his men fled in confusion. Pursued by over-whelming numbers, they were mostly made prisoners, while many were driven into the river to find a watery grave. In this extremity,

Leicester, with his remaining supporters, formed themselves into a compact mass, and the assailants, by extending their flanks, entirely surrounded them. With the determination of valiant warriors they refused to yield to "dogs and perjurers, and suffered themselves to be battered to pieces on the spot." Their bodies were piled in one hideous mass, while their red gore streamed down the tranquil vale as rain flowing in the street. Thus the night closed in, and the Prince's victory was completed.

It was approaching the cool hour of midnight, when three figures were seen crossing the vale that had just witnessed such bitter contention. Thousands of battered corpses blocked their way; men of might and renown, whose deeds were blotted out from remembrance. The lightning still flickered in the distant sky at rapid intervals, causing the ghastly remains that strewed the ground to appear and disappear like spectres in the night. The shouts of triumph that drowned the cries of the wounded had died away, while Sandford, with Morton and De Ardernne, traverse the fatal field. It was still a vexed question whether the great Earl of Leicester, whose iron sway had ruled kings and princes, existed. Had he escaped—or did his life-blood mingle with the red stream that stained the grassy hills? Not a word was uttered, but in breathless anxiety the shattered victims are diligently examined.

At length Morton stooped down, and discovered the surcoat bearing the device of his late master; part of his arms and accoutrements were also thrown in a careless heap. The young retainer pointed out these relics; a vivid stream of lightning shot across the heavens, its light disclosed the broken armour and mangled trunk of that powerful man, though the hands, feet, and head are gone. By whom this savage excess of human vengeance was perpetrated, has been, and ever will remain, a mystery. The head arrived at Wigmore Castle a few days after, as a present to Lady Mortimer, while the trunk, by the King's desire, was interred under the steps leading to the high altar at Evesham Abbey.

Without pretending to discuss the merits or demerits of this wonderful man, it is strange to observe how his death converted the sinner into the saint. Numbers flocked to the well near which his body was found, and pretended to be cured of divers diseases by drinking of its waters, others only needed to touch his tomb, or to apply the fillet to their forehead with which the departed warrior's frame had been measured. But the imagination has always a powerful influence on human disorders. In the present day many people are troubled with diseases of the fancy. They declare themselves better for a sip of the waters of Bath or Tonbridge, when nobody was

able to discover anything previously the matter
with them.   The nervous system has been
aroused from a state of *ennui* by a change of
scene and action ; a benefit, which in the darker
ages of superstition would, no doubt, have been
attributed to the working of some supernatural
agency.   But the night air is cold, and Sandford
with his companions are suffering from the excessive fatigues of this trying day.

" It is the King's command that I should conduct you to his presence," said De Ardernne,
addressing Sandford; "my duty is a pleasant
one, when I shall witness the highest honours
given to one whose ancestors formerly rendered
me great service that I have been unable to
requite."

" I was not conscious of obligations between
us," replied Sandford; " nor do I wish to inquire
into them.   Is my lord the King at the Abbey?
It is said he is wounded."

"It is but slight," answered De Ardernne; "the healing balms that the holy fathers possess will soon restore his strength. If rumour is correct, you are to depart for Guildford on the morrow."

"And shall I have the honour of travelling under your commands?" said Saudford.

"You jest with me," replied De Ardernne. "I should be but a serving man in the regal train with which you will be entrusted. There is other game afloat where I may play my part. I shall hence away to Kenilworth."

"To demand the surrender of the Castle to the King, I venture to presume," said Sandford; "should it be refused, I would then ask a favour of that friend, who is not forgetful of ancestral obligations."

"It is to your father I owe my life; when Richard, Earl Marshal, was forced to flee to Ireland," answered De Ardernne; "but what would you ask of me?"

" If Kenilworth refuses to capitulate," returned Sandford; "warn the detested Knight Rochfort de Vere that his possessions at Hurstingham, filched from De Meudon, are conferred upon myself, and that I demand instant surrender."

" It shall be as you wish," said De Ardernne; "though it would seem more consistent with discretion if he remained where he is."

" I have prepared to intercept him, should he dare to leave Kenilworth," replied Sandford. " Heaven is just, and I am desirous to forbear what may lead to further bloodshed."

" Your purpose may be well conceived," said De Ardernne; " but why spare one who has sworn to take your life?"

" I will bear no malice," replied Sandford. " He shall answer for his crimes before the King. However many murders he may have committed, I do not desire to avenge them by the perpetration of another."

"I will not fail to give your message," said De Ardernne; "though beware lest he should away to Hurstingham, and close its gates against you to the last extremity."

It merely remains to be recorded, that arrived at the Abbey, where the King was reposing, attended by numerous favourites, Sandford was conducted by the Prince into the Royal presence, and received the honour of Knighthood for his services. It was a distinction gained by the earnestness of his zeal. A great barrier was now removed, but all is not yet gained. He would almost have foregone the honours that had been bestowed to be assured of the Lady Emmeline's freedom from care and anxiety. The newly created Knight was haunted with apprehensions, which the last few eventful days did not enable him to subdue. But the extermination of the King's enemies left him at liberty. He was no longer a banished wanderer, in terror at the sound

of every horse's hoof that met his ear. Restless
and feverish with recent excitement, he is kindly
accommodated with a bed of rushes by a
sympathising father of Evesham. Sleep on,
bold youth, and take your rest, for one beloved
fair yet needs your manly succour.

After one day of necessary repose, Sandford,
surrounded by a gallant troop of warriors, started
for Guildford. His breast swelled with honest
emotion of hope, though mingled with fear.
Heaven had smiled on him in adversity, would
its watchfulness cease in prosperity? No. The
cause of the righteous shall flourish. Armed with
his patent of Knighthood, and the attainder on
the domains at Hurstingham, he speeds gaily
away. Onward still, to seek the prize for which
his heart had long and vainly sighed.

CHAPTER V.

"Nay, if the gentle spirit of moving words
  Can no way change you to a milder form,
  I'll woo you like a soldier at arms' end,
  And love you against the nature of love—force you."
                                        SHAKESPEARE.

ALONE from day to day in her chamber at
Pevensel, sat the Lady Emmeline. As both the
guardian and the maiden had bound themselves
to forbear any allusion to the subject uppermost
in their respective minds, it may be imagined
that all conversation between them had lately
been of a very ordinary character. The tender

damsel had abandoned all hope of again meeting
the one to whom her heart was endeared during
Savoy's lifetime. Yet constant in devotion, she
doted silently during the long hours of solitude,
while the peculiar times rendered her life one of
continued seclusion. Under these circumstances
the domestic, that had served her mistress for
some years with marked fidelity, rose almost to
the dignity of a companion, rather than a servant.

In this position of confidence, the zealous
coadjutor indulged great anticipations of Lady
Emmeline's union with Sandford, sooner or later.
But unhappily she could not rest satisfied to
ponder this cherished idea in her own breast.
One after another, the secret was confided amongst
the inferiors in the Castle; and with that exag-
geration which a story never fails to gain by
repetition, it is soon whispered from ear to ear as
an accomplished certainty, nor did the delusion

fail to become known to Savoy himself. The noble lord succeeded in tracing the report to its source, and it was on the fourth morning following the frightful scenes detailed in our last chapter that Emmeline was deeply moved to find her favourite servant in tears, when her manner had hitherto been so hopeful and free from remorse.

"What sudden trouble can thus choke your utterance, my faithful Anne?" said Emmeline. "Have you lost some dear friend? Open your heart to me, and remember that trouble is often a dew showered from heaven to refresh our affections for things to come."

"It is not what I have lost, but what I am to lose," replied the maid. "Oh! say wherein I have offended, deal not so harshly with one who has no friend on earth. It is indeed a sorry recompense for years of honest service. Why thus cast aside without just reason? I cannot leave you. Oh! once and for ever farewell!"

" If not possessed by some witch I entreat you to say what has happened," exclaimed Emmeline, quite bewildered. "Your fidelity shall not go unrequited. I am a friend, if my sympathy is worth acceptance. Have I ever dealt unkindly that you forsake me without cause or pretence?"

" Then it is not my lady's wish to discard me?" replied Anne. " In what have I incurred my lord's displeasure? He desires me to quit the Castle this night, and another is appointed in my place. Oh! my beloved mistress, speak a word in my lord's ear, suffer me not to be thrust friendless on the wide world, when I am ready to serve you while a spark of life is left within my body."

" I will be plain with you, Anne," returned Emmeline. " It has not escaped my notice. The favours I have shown excite the jealousy of your fellow servants. If in unguarded moments you have spoken of my future hopes, though innocent the intention, such actions have given them a weapon to use for your destruction, to my endless discomfort. No other subject would arouse the bitterness of my uncle's resentment."

" I may deserve my lady's reproof," answered Anne; "but my crime scarcely merits such severity. Will you speak for me? My lord is alone in his chamber."

"If truly convinced of your error," said Emmeline, " I will do my best; but there is an unhappy fact I cannot conceal. My influence with your lord has much depreciated since recent disclosures. It is cruel to make you answerable for my affections, and I can scarce express which would be grieved the most at such a parting, the mistress or the maid."

" Oh ! thank you ten thousand times," ejaculated Anne. " And may I be your attendant on this contemplated journey, or, if my lord travels alone, shall I remain still your constant servant in the Castle ?"

" I am not anticipating any journey in such dangerous times," replied Emmeline. " My uncle has never mentioned the subject, nor will I consent to quit this stronghold on any pretence; you are under some delusion."

" Not so, my dear mistress," rejoined the maid. " The necessary cavalcade is to be ready by the morning, and a litter is prepared for my lady. About a hundred of our best men are to march in the train."

" You have almost stunned me with this intelligence," cried Emmeline, trembling violently. " Am I to be dragged away against my will like a thief? Oh, heaven! grant the blessing of your protection. Some deep misery will befall your unhappy child, greater than any she has yet endured."

" Whatever calamities may overtake my lady," said Anne, " I only ask to share them. My lord will surely never be deaf to your entreaties;

there was a time when his heart would leap for joy, his venerable eyes sparkle to humour every little fancy of your childish whims. All is sadly changed, yet sympathy cannot entirely wear away as years steal upon our lives."

"Then I will seek my uncle at once, and intercede for you," said Emmeline. "Let me beg you will better rule the tongue in future. I am in a strait most painful. To leave this castle will break a solemn promise to one in whose judgment I have implicit confidence. To refuse, I violate an equally sacred engagement to my guardian. Entreaties may remove your troubles, but I know my guardian's will is stern, and I must plead hard for my own safety."

As Savoy endeavoured to meditate on the events which had taken place during his illness, his ideas resolved themselves into a peculiar state of chaotic jumble. There was no one to afford a proper explanation, so he looked solely to circum-

stantial evidence presented by facts that had subsequently occurred. Truly his niece had claimed
the honour of relieving the castle for one on
whose behalf she was naturally biassed, but when
the prisoners arrived, who had been forwarded
for safe custody by De Meudon (whose end was
yet of course unknown) the noble lord instantly
credited the young knight and the murdered
seaman with all the renown.

So vastly did this old man's mind vacillate, as
misconception followed misconception. The young
knight was all in all. He had attended the
Queen in Flanders. That royal lady desired
the presence of his niece on a matter concerning
her happiness. How irresistibly the two circumstances came together. The way to Guildford
was clear. He had men at arms to guard the
train. He had the watchful enemy safe in custody. Now was the golden chance to beat that
phantasy from the brain of a foolish girl. The

smiles of royalty, the persuasions of many courtly ladies, would soon lead her to despise what she had hitherto adored as perfection. Silly, childish whim, conceived in seclusion, which, owing to disordered times, had been prolonged beyond the years of infancy. Now the gay world is before her. So did Savoy's rambling thoughts paint images of an ideal future.

On quitting her chamber, Lady Emmeline was soon convinced of the correctness of her maid's assertions. There were unmistakable signs of preparation for the departure ; packs, ready to be conveyed by strong chargers, lay piled in regular heaps. The very sight of them filled that maiden breast with terror. Those words again sounded in her ear, "remain close within the castle." What a mysterious influence they had upon her senses—she thought of them with a shudder. There is no time to be lost—to-morrow morning she might be ruined for ever—to-night would bid farewell to that genuine creature who had shared her long hours of suspense. The girl's spirits rose with the emergency, and in mingled feelings of fear and indignation she sought her uncle's presence. Why—why had all been concealed from her until the last moment?

"Come hither, my child," said Savoy, "I have many things to speak which I deferred until you could better endure them. The Queen desires your presence. It is high time to throw off the simple girl, and become the courtly lady. And if I promised not to coerce, it is my plain duty to convince you of all former errors. Prepare, then, to leave for Guildford at daybreak."

"Oh, uncle, it is in my simplicity alone that I find happiness," said Emmeline. "How often should I have been utterly lost, had not another stronger in mind and body watched over me, guided by heaven's good will? Think well before you act. Emaciated by sickness, your frame is far too weak to endure a journey beset with danger at every step."

"You will not dissuade me," answered Savoy. "All is safe. That worthy young Knight, whose love you so unjustifiably despised, has cleared the way. To-morrow you must and shall leave the Castle. The Queen awaits our presence, and her commands shall not be violated to please the fancy of a presuming youth."

"Nay, then, forgetful of all promises, do you propose to compel me into an alliance with De Meudon?" replied Emmeline. "Not all the Queens in Europe could exact my willing consent. But I will be truthful. Our good deliverer did enjoin me not to leave this home. I have every faith in his judgment, nor can I venture to think you will force tyranny so far as to drag me away against my will."

"This insolent presumption will drive me to madness," said Savoy. "I claim to be best

judge of what is prudent, and what impossible.
Forbear, I say, or should I meet that youth again
it should be his death.   I demand your obedience,
and if words cannot bring back the milder form
which once existed within you I will try force.
Go and prepare for the morrow—no more I say,
or my senses will leave me."

"Oh! uncle," cried Emmeline, "if you still
love me withdraw that stern command.   We do
well to trust, but not to tempt, Providence.   Think
what storms of terror befel me, when all was an
apparent calm.   Let the past guide the future.
Wait at least a few days, when tidings of the
distant battles may cast all your imaginations to
the ground."

"I have delayed too long already," said Savoy.
"Nor will I argue with a foolish, dreaming
child.   You have dared me too far; refuse my
peremptory commands once more, and I will
follow that detested youth to the end of the

world. A banished wretch that shall die the death he merits."

"Oh! uncle, uncle," cried Emmeline, sinking upon her knees, and covering her face with both her hands, while her voice faltered between broken and frightful sobs, "you overtax the tenderness of womanly nature. If I must go with you— oh! heaven hear my prayer—frustrate the designs of evil men, and guide all things aright. I call your righteousness to be my witness. It is not my will that consents to this rash adventure. If my sins deserve these bitter chastisements—yet in mercy withhold thy frown, and let the sun which sets to-day in sorrow, rise joyfully on a smiling morn."

After a short pause, Savoy gently raised the agitated maiden, and held her in his arms. All his old love returned with this concession, trusting it was the preface to a still greater one. He kissed her heated cheeks, and endeavoured to administer the only consolation deemed likely to prove effectual.

"Remember, my beloved child, that nothing is so pleasing to heaven as obedience. Have confidence in my affection, and it will bring a happiness the fancies you have lately indulged can never afford."

"If I obey it is not from choice," answered Emmeline. "I could not endure the thought of violence; sooner would I perish. If I am lost remember my last words shall bless you, and implore the consolation of heaven on your broken heart, for broken it must be, should the horror of coming ruin overtake me."

"My poor child, be not so apprehensive," said Savoy; "once safe at Guildford, your eyes will open to a new world. Though grown to womanhood you are yet in the infancy of life."

"Where for the present I would wish to remain," replied Emmeline. "There have I found happiness, while but slight acquaintance with the outer world has been one scene of misery—oh! that I could live the days of childhood over again. Its merry hours often haunt the thoughts in days of care. And senseless to all worldly peril it laughs the playful moments away."

"Truly so," said Savoy, "though unconscious that its cares are not dispelled, but simply borne by others. And now, my child, let us prepare for this auspicious journey. Have you any request to make?"

"I have a question to ask," replied Emmeline. "In what has Anne so displeased you? She is a faithful creature, and scarcely merits such punishment. If I follow my question by a request, it is that she may be my attendant on this painful journey."

"She is a silly tattler," said Savoy, "and has brought evil upon her own head; but at your petition I will forgive thus far. She shall remain here during our absence. I have arranged with another to attend you at Guildford."

"And pray who may that be?" asked Emmeline.

"It is the poor widow, Rosanne Portevin," continued Savoy. "All her late husband's property has been pillaged. She is a beggar, and has the greatest claim on our protection."

"Disagreeable as she is, I grant her claim upon us," returned Emmeline. "By the obedience I am about to show, let me implore you to give her some other post. I could not bear that woman near me—nay, I would sooner travel alone."

"It is too late, my word is passed," said Savoy; "once more let me ask you to believe that oldest heads are the wisest. Anne's foolish tongue at Guildford would soon expose your recent follies,"

"And, indeed, I am not ashamed of them,"

answered Emmeline. " Yet I will engage to insure her silence. It is a trifling request, though one that will greatly comfort a heart overburdened with fear. If I go with you, it is under the influence of greater terror at your anger, than at my probable fate. It may seem a fancy, but let Anne go with us, a matter that cannot be prejudicial."

" It may be a little matter to you, but a great one to me," replied Savoy. " It grieves me to refuse, but I have solid reasons that your innocent mind may not comprehend. I have already agreed for her to remain here, and vex me not by repeated requests that may necessitate the withdrawal of any concessions."

" I say no more, though it is a mystery to me to be thus distrusted," answered Emmeline. " Good night, my fondest guardian; remember me in your prayers, as I will think of you. It will be a longing glance that I shall cast back at

these olden walls. Heaven grant I may visit
them again in safety and honour. This is to me
a sorry, sorry day."

It is night. A fond farewell is spoken between
a thoughtful mistress and a watchful maid. A
farewell that seemed like two loving hearts parting for ever in this world. Oh, that the gallant,
who dashes boldly across the country leading a
warlike band, could behold that picture of maiden
terror. The men at arms are confident in their
strength ; there is only one, the rejected domestic,
who shares her mistress's apprehensions. They
may be shadows—they may be realities—still
they haunt the mind. What dangers had hitherto
been passed unscathed, but they had been overcome by the energies of one whose injunctions
were to be disregarded for the first time. Bitterly
the tender girl ponders on this predominating
thought; oh ! heaven—thou alone knowest the
issue of all things—calm those fears, assuage

the troubles of a racked and divided mind. She would yet remain, but dare not. Would the fond youth forgive her imprudence? Yes; and still bring aid in the hour of need, but the faithful Conisburgh is gone also, her peril must remain unknown.

It is morning; no Rosanne Portevin has appeared. All is ready for the start. There is another mystery in the changing winds. The last moment is come, and Anne, wild with joy, is permitted to attend her mistress on the emergency. The outer walls are passed; Emmeline cast one sad look upon those fading towers. Onward the cavalcade wends its way. Every leaf that rustled in the winds sent a chill through the maiden's frame; but not a hostile footstep trod their path. All is silent; all is still, save the clatter of horses' hoofs, which only ceased when, halting beside some murmuring stream, the animals sip its refreshing element; and, like its

flowing waters, the hours glide away, until the
silver moon broke through the dark clouds of
evening, and shed a light serene upon the advancing travellers. It seemed to blot out the thought
of calamity as the opaque vapours melt before its
tender beams.

Both man and horse are weary, and the night
is still advancing upon them. A few troopers
ride in advance, and winding their hoarse
trumpets, they request hospitality at the Castle
at Knep. This stronghold, situated about five
miles south of Horsham, was then held by
William de Browse, whose absence was amply
atoned for by the kind attention of his principal
officers. Only a small remnant of one tower
remains at this day to mark the spot where an
anxious maiden spent this eventful night. The
noble Lord is, of course, honoured with the
principal guest chamber, while the men content
themselves with a temporary bivouac in the outer

court. But there is a morrow yet to come. Sleep, gentle lady; the morning flowers have not yet bloomed to greet your onward course. The winds are still; is there no sound of an approaching storm? The day is passed in safety, let the morrow take thought for itself.

CHAPTER VI.

" Crabbed age and youth
  Cannot live together ;
Youth is full of pleasure,
  Age is full of care :
Youth like summer morn,
  Age like winter weather."
                    The Passionate Pilgrim.

IT was on the morn preceding the departure
from Pevensel that Rosanne Portevin, having
entered into an engagement with Savoy, departed
to Seaford, for the purpose of administering some
sound advice to her skittish daughter, who was
then located with the departed father's brother.

This cross-grained woman had contracted a religious antipathy against all youthful affections. The little passages of love between Kitty and Conisburgh, a source of constant jest to the tattlers of the Castle, burnt like red hot coals on the fire of indignation that raged within the mother's breast. Frown upon frown clouded her sullen brow, only to afford greater merriment to the jesters.

Under promise to return that night, old Rosanne successfully crossed the lofty downs which intercept the Port of Seaford from Pevensey, and trudged on to the hut serving for her brother-in-law's abode. Its rudeness contrasted unfavourably with the old house at Hastings. Large chinks in the decaying walls enabled the anxious mother to scrutinize the interior with some tolerable approach to accuracy, though the door was barred against her, and the loudest exclamations failed to provoke any reply.

There was a fair that attracted the inhabitants of the Port, who availed themselves of its facilities to procure articles of domestic use, which these institutions at the time afforded the only opportunity to obtain that occurred during the year. Jugglers and other showmen plied their trade with energy and success. The scowl that hung on Rosanne's face was the prevailing subject of mimicry; but no Kitty is there. Strange that her merry little humours should not be attracted by these tomfooleries.

With temper still rising, the old woman proceeded to the shore. It is low water. The port being left high and dry, comparatively speaking, and the rude vessels tumbling on their sides like defunct teetotums. At last a small pinnace approached from a vessel that lay waiting a favourable wind to spread its sails. It contained a stout, burly figure, and a little maid whose form could not be mistaken. Kitty soon skipped out of the boat, but the burly man, having once met his sister-in-law, had ever since regarded her with an instinctive horror. After landing his charge, he pushed off from the shore with a rapidity that could not have been exceeded had a modern hydra or a rabid Cerberus awaited him.

" Come ashore to see this foolish fair, I suppose, you silly child?" said Rosanne. " Strange that people can't buy what they need without looking on this mummery. Not happy until you got away from home; perhaps you will be more contented still to learn there's no home left."

" If you have sold everything in a pet, I must be content with a roving life," answered Kitty. " My uncle is gone to Spain, and I was returning to Hastings this very day to see old friends again."

" I don't suppose you were coming to see me," said Rosanne. " Ruin is come upon us;

I have taken service with the Lord of Pevensel, and leave you to fight the world, instead of listening to love nonsense prated by a servant. Go, then, to Hastings, and see what old friends will do who robbed me of every scrap belonging to your dead father directly the breath was out of his body."

" It is impossible," said Kitty; " my father's companions would find a home for his little girl that amused them for many a dull hour."

" Foolish girl," returned Rosanne; " they were glad enough to drink your father's wine, and to be the spectators of your childish tricks. Try them now in our adversity. I should have been mulcted of everything, had I not concealed some coins under my dress."

" Oh! mother, why have you withheld this from me?" replied Kitty. " I am alone and friendless. Uncle is gone; this veering wind has filled his sails. Where—where shall I go?"

"So you begin to feel the consequence of being guided by an obstinate father," retorted Rosanne. "Perhaps you had better try and find this Conisburgh, though do not imagine he will care much about you now."

"I fear not, even in this extremity," replied Kitty; "you, mother, could not expect a kindness. A friendly voice never won your smiles, or a pleasant word your cheerful answers. Return to Pevensel, and I will find a path if the world is twice as rugged as you represent."

"Then come not crying to me in a few days," said Rosanne. "I travel to Guildford in the morning with the Lord of Pevensel, and his niece. You will soon learn the worth of a mother's care."

"Nay, mother, I should always have loved you better had I not lived in fear," rejoined Kitty. "Forget not that you still have a child. Life is short. Let us try to lighten its burden.

I may be young and thoughtless; but if youth is not gay, wherein would age find pleasure; come —let us love as becomes parent and child."

This childish rebuke was not without its effect even on so strong a heart as Rosanne's. She dreaded the consequence of leaving that helpless girl alone at the mercy of any villain that might cross her path. How could she help her unhappy offspring? Lady Emmeline's attendant was to be dismissed. Might not Kitty be more suitable than herself for such a post? and the noble Lord would, perhaps, be induced to confer another position in his Castle. It might be tried, but not to-night, because she knew Savoy would be disinclined at first to such a proposal. In prosperity Rosanne never indulged a thought or care for others, but, at the last moment, her sternness yielded at the sight of her child cast forth on the desert of the wide, wide world.

" No, I cannot leave you thus, with all your

faults," said Rosanne. " We will try and find
some sympathetic travellers who will be returning
to Lewes this night. Go with them, Kitty, and
meet the cavalcade from Pevensel, at the stone in
Fletching forest. I am sure my Lord will permit
you to proceed with us for your father's sake."

" I will obey you, dear mother," said Kitty.
" But do not despise that good youth, Conisburgh. I am sure he will assist us in this
matter."

" Heaven knows where he is," said Rosanne.
" Long since he was sent away with his adventurous master; if you think of nothing but that
silly love dream, I cannot help you. That name
must not be mentioned in the Castle."

" In what has he offended the noble Lord,
then ?" said Kitty.

" I know nothing of it, and care less," said
Rosanne. " Only remember that for speaking
that young man's name, or his master's, within

Lady Emmeline's hearing, her attendant, Anne, is discarded; so keep your flighty little tongue still."

" Poor Anne! it seems impossible," replied Kitty; " the gentle lady quite loved her. She cannot know it, and will yet prevail upon her uncle to relent. But, for better or for worse, I will be at the cross at Fletching wood to-morrow. Shall I see you there, dear mother, for certain ?"

" The noble Lord will not repent when a foolish whim is to be beaten from his niece's imagination," said Rosanne. " The master has stuffed her brain with the same folly that the man has conjured into yours. Think no more of it; pro- , bably you will never see him again."

" Oh! I cannot believe it," said Kitty; " the noble Lord would never forget who saved his castle from destruction."

" And consigned your father to his grave," answered Rosanne; " betrayed him to serve his

own selfish ends. Villain! he merits death itself,
and is rightly rejected as a presuming adventurer."

When matters arrived at this crisis, Kitty
deemed it better to smother her thoughts, and
quietly acquiesced in all her mother's directions.
It was nearly dark before an arrangement was
concluded with some townspeople returning to
Lewes for the little maid's conveyance. So the
mother and child parted. Though nothing shook
the gaiety of her young spirit, Kitty pictured her
mother as taking a longer journey over the wild
downs in the gloom of night. She would be at
Lewes before her last remaining parent reached
Pevensel. Aye, there is often truth in the passing
fancy of uncertain thoughts! It was a longer
journey, leading to loftier regions than those
towering downs that gradually faded in the mist
of night. There, wandering still, the newly-
appointed attendant gropes her way; then sud-

denly she arrived at a pit dug out of the solid
chalk of which the hills are composed. She
started on the very verge, and shuddered from
head to foot. The overhanging ground crumbled
beneath her weight, and the rest is a momentary
and whirling chaos ;—a violent storm that
occurred shortly afterwards brought down more
of the broken ground, completely burying the unhappy mother, and some months elapsed before
the pit was ready to obtain ballast for ships.
Then the mystery was solved, and Rosanne was
recognised by the bags of coin still concealed
under the clothes that covered her rotted corpse.

Having reached Lewes in safety, Kitty started
on the following morning to seek the stone in
Fletching wood. The forest afforded every facility
for concealment. There hour after hour passed
before the tramping of horses sounded gradually
louder and louder as they approached the land-
mark. They come, but the little maid did not.

venture from her hiding place, intending to rush out as her mother passed. At last, with a start of amazement, she beheld the Lady Emmeline, and, strange as it seemed, attended by the ever faithful Anne.

" Yet it is easily accounted for," thought Kitty ; " the lady's entreaties have induced her uncle to let Anne be her attendant, while Rosanne Port-evin remained at Pevensel. It must be so, and no doubt I am to go with them."

Before the little maid could summon resolution to make her appearance, the rear of the cavalcade had almost reached the stone where she waited. A gallant man, who recognised her, dismounted, placed the lighter burden on the horse, and led the animal a short distance behind his com-panion.

" Her mother had not since appeared at Pevensel—a deeper mystery, but one which so gay a mind would soon paint into a bright picture. Her mother travel to Guildford—it was an invention! She had merely acted for the sake of her child, thinking that if once she could be brought under Savoy's notice, some good post in the Castle would be bestowed in consideration of her late father's exertions."

In this frame of mind she laughed the hours gaily away, though possessed by a timidity to which her sprightly nature was formerly quite strange. She did venture to make her presence known, and, following, entered the Castle at Knep. There she reposed in a separate apartment, while both Savoy and his niece continued ignorant of the accession to their train.

CHAPTER VII.

"A loss of her
That, like a jewel, has hung twenty years
About his neck, yet ne'er lost her lustre."
SHAKESPEARE.

IF the area occupied by the little Castle of Knep was somewhat limited, and especially so to those who were accustomed to the more extensive stronghold of Pevensel, Savoy would soon have been compensated for the deficiency, had the castles his imagination built in vacancy during that night been realised in actual fact. Probably his mind, impaired both by age and recent bodily

F 5

sickness, was wandering considerably astray. But sleeping or waking he passed the time away in visionary delusions. He conceived his niece the bride of some lordly baron, whose domain far exceeded either Pevensel or Kenilworth in extent and magnificence. The journey to Guildford was to accomplish this, and perhaps more. How easy can the conceptions picture what the heart would desire! as many at this day struggle with the world's greatest misfortunes, doting upon some brilliant prospect that the future is to open. So hope in its flighty moment becomes the germ of disappointment;—a seed thrown on rocky ground, and scattered by the wind in one short hour.

But to Lady Emmeline all seemed dark as the light which surrounded her lonely bed. She looked back, and not forward. She longed to see again those massive towers so associated with the days of childish innocence, with a happy girlhood and the early years of matured beauty. Why had she left them? to please the imaginations of pride. Truly, there was no danger outwardly apparent, though again a still small voice whispered constantly in her ear, "Remain close within the Castle." Yet all seemed safe. But may not the most gallant bark plough the rampant waves, and fly gaily on their surging foam to be crushed in a moment by some hidden danger nigh? It is too late to repent when the morrow cannot undo the evil of to-day. The simplicity of Emmeline's nature rendered her powers of endurance almost inexhaustible, and the heaviness that remained from the night, oppressing her maiden breast, brought peace and hopefulness in the morning, though mingled with uncertainty and remorse. There was one far away, whose fate she still conceived as trembling in an evenly balanced scale, that one adverse breath would weigh to the ground for ever.

After passing the night in sound sleep, which
fatigue had rendered essential, Kitty, awakened
by the fresh air of morn, rose gaily with the lark.
She had hitherto followed in the train unobserved, but it would be impossible to leave the
little Castle on resuming the journey without the
knowledge of Savoy or his niece. The little maid
determined at once to confess the truth to Lady
Emmeline. Having ascertained that her mother
was expected to be the lady's attendant, and
though she deemed her previous conjectures on
this subject erroneous, yet, impelled by the liveli-
ness of her spirits, she even jested at the thought
of her parent losing her way on the downs at
night, and so failing to reach Pevensel in time
for the departure, which took place at the first
gleam of daylight.

But the innocent girl was little conscious of
the complications to which her presence would
give rise. The tattler had been busy at Pevensel,

and the very reason that induced Savoy to select
Rosanne Portevin as a watch dog over his niece
would constitute an insuperable objection to poor
little Kitty. The noble Lord had heard of her
flirtations with Conisburgh; and as that young
man was altogether discarded from his favour, it
may be supposed that the skittish girl would only
be regarded as another medium of communication to Sandford,—an offence that doomed poor
Anne to dismissal, though born and bred in the
Castle, and ignorant of the world beyond its
walls.

The little orphan knocked gently at the lady's
chamber, while both Emmeline and her maid
were engaged in devotion. There was no response.
By-and-bye she heard a movement. The little
modest tap is repeated; but before the door
could be unlatched, Savoy's footsteps echoed
down the vaulted passage. Kitty vanished like
a water sprite, and Anne opened the door to gaze

on nothing but stone walls. When the coast was clear the intruder returned, and on being admitted Anne turned deadly pale, either from fear or surprise, perhaps both; and the lady could not have opened her eyes wider had Sandford appeared in familiar shape.

"My poor child, where is your mother?" said Emmeline; "and why thus venture to follow us? Do not deceive me, or disguise anything, however terrible."

"Forgive me, dear lady," answered Kitty, making a profound courtesy. "I am alone and friendless, but I will not deceive my lady. I am trying to reach Guildford to find my mother; some will pity a lone and penniless girl."

"What, have you no protector on earth?" said Emmeline. "Has everyone deserted you in this extremity? Come, tell me all."

"I left my mother at Seaford, and believe she lost her way in crossing those wild downs at night," replied Kitty. "I cannot return to Pevensel alone; let me go with you. I have only one other friend on earth who may pity me."

At this last sentence Kitty blushed deeply.

"Those red cheeks tell a tale," said Anne. "It will be ruin if my Lord should find you here—I should get all the blame. Oh! for heaven's sake go back!"

"That is impossible, Anne," answered Emmeline. "The poor girl would soon be lost in these desolate woods. I will speak to my uncle. He will not cast the poor orphan aside, whose father perished in his cause; but who is the friend that brings the crimson blood to your face—is it a lover?"

"My dear mistress," said Anne. "God forbid that I should wish to act harshly to this desolate child. It is a lover she speaks of, the good man Conisburgh. But your uncle knows it, and he would deem this poor girl's presence more objectionable than ever."

"You bewilder me," answered Emmeline; "when and where are these troubles to end? I dare not speak of her; but we cannot cast her forth alone, perhaps to fall into brutal hands and come to ruin. Unhappy girl, like myself your path seems choked with thorns. Anne, what are we to do?"

"She must follow behind the cavalcade," said Anne; "and we will try to find her service at Guildford. Go now, my lady, and seek your uncle, or he may anticipate by coming to this chamber. We are acting most imprudently, though our intentions may be innocent."

These arrangements being made, Lady Emmeline had only just passed out of the chamber before she accosted Savoy, who was making his way to her apartment. They returned to the guest chamber, both silently occupied in meditations. But in the morning rumour had already got afloat, and the noble lord began to suspect that the absence of Rosanne Portevin was not attributable to accident, and coupling this circumstance with her daughter and Conisburgh, he now seriously doubted whether the old woman was worthy of the confidence he intended to place in her. He firmly believed she had been kept out of the way for Anne's benefit, and after remaining at Pevensel until he returned, she would doubtless have some plausible excuse to offer in extenuation of her conduct. As these thoughts shot across his mind they gave rise to new determinations. He foreshadowed a vast change to be worked by the Queen's influence, and considering that his niece's mind would become flexible if surrounded by entirely new faces, he resolved to leave her at Guildford with the Queen, and to return to Pevensel with all his train, including Anne herself. So one imagination upon another rose in the noble lord's breast, only to vanish like apparitions the nearer they were approached.

"I beg of you, nay, I insist, that you tell everything concerning this Rosanne Portevin's absence," said Savoy. "I trusted you, and on that account agreed to let Anne come with us at the last moment, and once more I will not countenance or endure the slightest deception."

"You accuse me most wrongfully, my dear uncle," said Emmeline. "I am quite innocent of that woman's non-appearance; it is really most unjust to hold me responsible for the offences of others."

"Then I am at a loss to comprehend it unless Anne is plotting without your knowledge," replied Savoy. "Some deception is being practised, for the woman's daughter was seen watching us in Fletching wood."

"I believe Anne quite incapable of such an

act," said Emmeline, endeavouring to suppress her fears. "She would never dream of attempting such a thing without my knowledge. Dismiss, I implore you, such suspicions from your mind. I have promised to go with you to Guildford, and Heaven grant we may reach our journey's end in safety."

"There is no doubt of it," rejoined Savoy; "if any danger did exist it must be long since passed. We have plenty of assistance to contend with such an emergency—it is incomprehensible that your thoughts should continue to dwell on such a subject—nothing but a childish fear."

"This day will show," answered Emmeline; " we have an ungovernable and wary foe to deal with, who may still be lurking in some secret hiding place, nor have we anyone to restrain them or to out-manœuvre their wicked designs. Heaven save us if I am right; but do beware how you proceed."

" You seem to treat me as a dotard," replied Savoy; "nor am I at a loss to conjecture who has crammed your brain with such a notion. It would almost appear that something is to happen on the road of which you have a certain knowledge. Perhaps you affect an unwillingness to leave Pevensel as a contrivance to hoodwink my senses."

" My dear uncle, your imaginations are most unreasonable," said Emmeline. " I would gladly return if it was not attended with greater danger than proceeding ; you misjudge all my motives. Believe then, once and for ever, that my confidence is not altered, even under the unhappy circumstances that surround me."

"The brightest prospects are before you, if your foolish young head could only believe it," replied Savoy; "unless there is some obstacle to arise of which you may be better aware than I am. It is my purpose to leave you at Guildford,

and to return to Pevensel with all the train.
Anne must also go back with us."

" Nay, surely you would let Anne remain with
me ?" answered Emmeline.

" I tell you no," said Savoy, interrupting her.
" My will is fixed and positive. I cannot suffer you
to be influenced by her foolish chatter, when you
must learn to mix with others suited to your
rank and manners. I do not wish to be stern or
unkind to her ; she shall remain at Pevensel, and
perhaps be restored to her position as your attendant at some future time."

" Uncle, have you really considered all these
plans ?" replied Emmeline. " You know there
are struggles proceeding that may crush every
hope we have in this world ; the issue may now
be decided, though not within the scope of our
knowledge. Our situation is one that must re-
quire the greatest caution."

" No more precautions are required than those

already taken," returned Savoy. "I am sanguine as to the result of impending battles, if, indeed, they have not already taken place. Permit me to say, that, old as I am, I deem myself capable of managing these affairs. You are but a weak vessel, and had better suffer those to guide you still who have reared you in safety from infancy."

"I do not wish to depreciate your kindness," said Emmeline, "but I cannot forget that I owe much of my safety to others."

"You are a wilful and obstinate girl," answered Savoy; "without directly breaking your vows in plain language, you do so in sinister hints, that are even more objectionable. It is better we should part for a time, and that you should be with others, who may gain more influence over your mind."

"I pray that your decision may have some good result," said Emmeline. "May I find joy

in the outer world as true and pure as my heart
would desire. Fear not that I shall become high-
minded or imaginative, or that my affections will
change. I believe this new beginning of my life
will only strengthen them, and perhaps convince
you they are not ill-considered."

" Peace, you silly child!" replied Savoy, who
could not suppress a smile at this vision of the
future so different to what he had painted. " A
few weeks may vastly alter your ideas, while
mine are fixed upon former experience. Go, now,
and prepare to re-commence this journey, and
when night leaves you time for solitary thought,
weigh my injunctions well in your heart. Once
more, and for the last time, let the past be looked
upon as a dream, and remember that wisdom
begins when folly ends."

With those who moralize on the proceedings
of others, it is a common fault to advance arguments that would apply with greater force to their

own acts, and often they forget that the tree of experience is frequently choked in its growth by the wild weeds of prejudice. It is difficult to remove the weakest barrier that stands between the mind and its cherished conceptions. Even when the deepest abyss of ruin is gaping before the sight, men still cling to the one thought that has so long possessed them. They seem incapable of drawing any new conclusions. Savoy at this moment was engrossed with one idea, against which no reason could prevail. Error upon error possessed him the further he advanced.

It was yet early on a bright August morning, when the cavalcade filed out of the little castle in the same order that it entered on the previous night. Savoy led the way, conversing with his officers concerning the probability of the war. In the centre came Emmeline and her attendant, again launched upon the quicksand of human casualties, and little Kitty, assisted by the same gallant retainer, followed behind at a respectful distance, that she could escape from observation if desirable. The path which they had to traverse was narrow, rendering a considerable elongation of the train indispensable. The greater part of the way was overgrown with moss and lichen, presenting a smooth and greasy surface, on which the animals maintained themselves on their hoofs with much difficulty. Here and there was a woodland cottage, rude and miserable in aspect, perhaps not more humble than the wretched serfs who found a dwelling within their walls, on whose faces there hung a sorrowful dejection, that years of oppression could alone have produced.

Under these difficulties the travellers made rather slow progress towards their destination ; but on arriving about two miles from Guildford, the ground was of a nature to permit the horses to proceed at a more rapid pace, when they reached a spot where another bye-road crossed the one on which they journeyed at an obtuse angle. Here the wily foes that had left their hiding-place near Pevensel found a suitable concealment. Drawn up in readiness they awaited the approaching cavalcade, and lay in ambush, unobserved, until the Lady Emmeline and her attendant arrived at the juncture of the roads. Then they dashed swiftly forward; they broke the centre of the train, and carried off the fair prize with her domestic, who, clinging to her swooning mistress, rent the forest with fearful shrieks. It was the work of a moment; a portion of the hostile band roughly removed the lady and servant, while the remainder engaged Savoy's men in a sanguinary encounter, about half-a-dozen on each side being slain. In the confusion all trace of the lady was lost, and numerous speculations arose as to the author of this violence.

As soon as all the enemy had escaped into the

forest, Savoy instituted a searching investigation into the occurrence. Had it happened nearer to Pevensel, he might have been willing to believe that Rochfort de Vere had left some watchers in ambush, besides those discovered by De Meudon. But such a notion seemed utterly improbable in the present locality. The one idea again forced itself uppermost in his mind—" The absence of Rosanne Portevin—her daughter watching in Fletching wood—there is foul play somewhere— had his niece really endured a calamity, or was she deceiving him still?" While in this doubting state of mind, he was informed that Kitty was seen at the rear of the cavalcade that morning, but was now missing. This at once afforded an imaginative solution of the mystery. The fair maiden had been carried off by Sandford and Conisburgh, and under that decided and erroneous impression Savoy continued the journey to Guildford, unable to realize the horror of his niece's situation. " Wretch !" the noble lord was often heard to exclaim. " I will have his heart's blood —vile, shameful plot—and much I fear my niece herself is not innocent in the matter." So, in burning indignation, Savoy reached the old place about two hours after noontide.

But with the unhappy maiden the horror of the position seemed only to come upon her by imperceptible degrees. There was a hopeless consciousness that she was lost for ever, and by her disregard of Sandford's instructions she looked upon the whole fabric of her life as fallen to the ground, and nothing remained but a dreary waste of terror and misery. Nor was her grief selfish ; she thought bitterly of other hearts besides her own that would be broken by this sad calamity. She commended herself to God ; and as she passed the woodland dingle, through which her captors led the way, bygone days flitted across her as one long dream. She reflected cheerfully

on her worldly career, as one that gave no re-
proach to mar her peace, no regret, except what
the acts of others had inflicted upon her. A
heavenly calmness possessed her disciplined and
innocent heart, even in the extremity of danger.

It was towards night before the full extent of
her peril was revealed. In the grey light of
evening the Castle of Hurstingham towered above
the surrounding country, and disclosed the fearful
fact. That horror, which for several months had
haunted the fair lady, now approached as a terrible
reality. Ah! well she remembered that spot in
happy days. It was in a playful hour when she
last quitted that stronghold; a little boy, whose
increased and manly form had lately been
stretched low on the field at Kenilworth, stole an
artful kiss as she mounted her pony. But such
joyful hours of mirth did not then await her.
She thought bitterly of Marion de Manville, her
old playmate, whose sufferings within those walls

no one was able to describe, and which perhaps
in a great measure would remain unknown, until
the great record of all human lives is opened.
She felt the unavailing emptiness of regrets, and
prayed for early termination of her sorrow.

As they approached the stronghold, it did not
escape Anne's observation that no banner floated
proudly on the lofty towers. This circumstance
denoted the absence of the lord himself. It might
perhaps be a slender hope, like a straw floating on
the pool within the grasp of a drowning man.
But slight as it was, it aroused some feelings of
relief in the domestic's mind. "A respite would
be afforded before the extreme of all evils could
befall them, and in that interval what measures
might be concerted for their succour? If only little
Kitty was aware of her mistress's situation it was
a great gain." This faithful servant roused herself to the emergency; she could be a comfort to
her mistress, if she could not save her; and as

the heavy portal of the Castle swung behind them, partly by entreaties and partly by offer of bribes, she succeeded in being allowed to occupy the same apartment as Lady Emmeline; and by determination she averted any attempt at violence by the inferiors in whose charge they were left. The various phases of hope and fear through which they passed will be a subject for future contemplation.

Some few hours after the excitement caused by the encounter in the forest had subsided Kitty ventured from the hiding place where she secluded herself during the struggle. All was still and calm. Nothing was visible in the shape of humanity, except the corpses of those who perished in the recent struggle. For the moment she gazed upon these lifeless forms with increasing terror. At last a small scroll of paper tucked in the girdle of one of the dead attracted her notice; she drew it gently out, and endeavoured in vain to decipher the written characters. She had, however, sense enough to imagine that it might contain some important information, and after securing it in her dress she trudged away to Guildford; but the numerous roads bewildered her without some guide, and night would probably have found her still wandering in the forest had she not met with a tanner, who plied his trade in the town she desired to reach. This good man took pity on the little lost sheep, and conveyed her in safety to the old palace, where she arrived about two hours after Savoy and his troop.

CHAPTER VIII.

"But lost, for ever lost to me those joys,
    Which reason scatters, and which time destroys ;
    No more the midnight fairy tribe I view,
    All in the merry sunshine tippling dew ;
    E'en the last fiction of the brain,
    The churchyard ghost, is now at rest again."

                                        CRABBE.

THOSE who would carp and cavil at the superstitions of former ages, should remember that there
are, at the present day, believers in fatality influenced by planets and other celestial phenomena.
There exists still a variety of outrageous forms of
religious delusion, which need not be particular-

G 5

ised, though, happily, the great truth will prevail. There has also recently arisen, during this enlightened age, a sect called the Peculiar People, who pretend to cure all manner of diseases by anointing with oil, despising all modern improvement, both in medical and ordinary intellectual progress; and if these delusions are entitled to some pity on the score of ignorance, how much greater allowance should be made for times when education was confined within the narrowest limits.

About two days had elapsed since the great struggle in the vale of Evesham. Black clouds, that obscured the sun's bright rays, hung their lowering vapours almost upon the towers of Kenilworth; and as night closed in, the blackened mass hovered still in the whirling air, disturbed by hollow and roaring winds. No dazzling planet shed its lustre upon the earth; the stars withheld their light, and prostrate upon the moistened ground lay a dying form, with vision closing from the passing signs of bright or clouded skies to behold new scenes that give no range for fancy or imagination, where all is certain and realized truth.

The light of day is gone. Through the thick forest where Conisburgh and his companions kept a patient watch the solemn winds murmured in sounds that seemed to whisper from unearthly regions. It seemed a fit accompaniment for ghostly apparitions, while the prostrate hag muttered in hollow tones a faint echo to the stirring elements. Here a little group of manly forms assembled ; one solitary torch shed a ruddy glare upon the haggard face before them, while Conisburgh stooped down over the dying woman to receive her blessings at that final and impressive moment.

" Mine hour is almost come," said Margot; " these dark clouds draw a veil over my life.

Young man, your time is yet to begin. A bright planet shone upon your birth, which again will sparkle in this nightly sky when I am far away; then will your future begin. Come near to me."

"Good mother, I am here," said Conisburgh; "but why are my fortunes to commence with the end of your life? Come, be more hopeful, we shall yet pass pleasant days together. Your poor son being lost, I am only endeavouring to supply his place."

"And worthily so," said Margot. "Born on the same day, the star that smiled on your first breath was hidden with clouds as thick as these above when my unhappy son first opened his eyes."

"And what follows, good mother?" said Conisburgh.

"That you become possessed of his birthright," answered Margot. "Look under the folds of my dress and find a parchment scroll; it is thine.

With my life these black vapours pass away; but
they speak also of vengeance, for the next clouded
sky is death to a greater sinner!"

"The scroll is here; tell me, mother, what
would you have done with it," answered Conisburgh. "I will be faithful to every wish you
may speak."

"Listen to me while I have breath to tell the
tale," said Margot. "On that scroll is recorded
certain exact spots of ground. There, with my
own hand, I buried large sums of treasure—one
in Hastings, the rest in France. All is thine;
for so the sign must be fulfilled."

"And what sign, good mother, will be fulfilled
if this treasure should come into my possession?"
replied Conisburgh.

"The sign of the stars that shone upon my
nativity," said Margot. "Its lustre was bright
and radiant; but presently a dark cloud obscured
its light, which opened in a small patch near the

centre. The little star peeped through like a maiden's eye at a lattice when her lover passes near. My life then was to be saved by a stranger who would inherit all my wealth."

"And who spoke of this star that shone upon you?" said Conisburgh.

"It was the dying words of my mother, as worthy of belief as the oath of the purest saint," replied Margot. "Now comes the chill and pouring rain to wash away my sins!"

At this moment the rain began to descend in torrents. It was requisite to remove the dying woman to a temporary hut constructed by Conisburgh and his companions. There they rested in turns; but the sleepers who occupied it were obliged to be aroused to make room for the expiring witch. This exertion almost brought the scene to a premature termination, somewhat to Conisburgh's dismay, as he was desirous of gaining further information concerning the buried treasure. This practice was much adopted in ages when the plunder of his goods was almost certain to follow the death or misfortunes of a Christian ; and Margot took this precaution when her husband departed from the world.

" Good mother, tell me this," said Conisburgh, when the old woman had slightly revived after her removal; "must I have complete faith in these signs to find this treasure ?"

" The sign is passed," answered Margot, " the substance is yet to come. It is all yours ; lay my body in some peaceful churchyard, that my ghost may not follow you. My eyes are closing fast ; are the clouds passed away, or do visions haunt my brain ?"

" The night is black as thunder, mother," said Conisburgh; "and the rain comes down in a torrent that almost washes the forest away."

" Then tell me no more," replied Margot. " Remember the scroll ; Heaven bless you."

"Farewell then, good mother," said Conisburgh. "I have endeavoured to be a friend."

A change passed over the old woman's countenance that caused Conisburgh to stop short in his utterance. Her breathing became short and cumbered. Her organs of vision were fixed as the star that shone at her birth. Her breast heaved heavily. Placing his head near, the young man listened attentively for three hours. There was but one slight convulsion more. The torrent of rain had ceased. The winds are hushed, all is calm and peace. The sky is studded with innumerable gems, but those glazed eyes do not behold them. Her imaginations, her flimsy shadows of prophetic utterance have vanished with the clouds.

It is probable that these superstitions were instilled into this woman during childhood. The hand of the assassin gave the death blow both to her husband and her son. These calamities affected her reason, and the imagination recalled the follies which excited terror and curiosity in the earliest days of life.

On the following morning, Conisburgh arranged with some rustics for the interment of this unhappy woman, whose remains were carried to a churchyard about five miles distant. There she laid in peace, and it is only to be regretted that such superstitions were not there and then interred with her bones.

It is possible that Conisburgh would have put very little faith in this woman's disclosures concerning this treasure, had not Kitty once mentioned that her father had strong suspicions on the subject. The scroll detailed the exact spot where each bag was secreted with the most minute correctness, the distance from the neighbouring trees was carefully noted, convincing the young man that once upon a time the old woman must have possessed management and reason of no common order, and she must have exercised considerable foresight in concealing this wealth. A tolerably clear proof that her eccentricities had been the growth of recent years.

Having lost his guard that watched the fortress at Kenilworth, Conisburgh was obliged to fill that office himself, and the old woman's remains had scarcely been carried away before a bustling scene at the gate of the Castle attracted his notice. It evidently foreshadowed some important occurrence.

CHAPTER IX.

" 'Tis ever thus
With noble minds, if chance they stoop to folly,
Remorse stings deeper, and relentless conscience
Pours more into the bitter cup
Of their severe repentance."

MASON.

ON the morning that Lady Emmeline fell into
the snare she had so long dreaded, a powerful
band of warriors halted about ten miles west of
Guildford, their horses being unable to proceed
in consequence of excessive fatigue. The commander, a newly created Knight, who had played

an important part in recent events, was much chagrined when this delay became an imperative necessity, and anxious that the Queen should have the earliest possible intelligence on matters wherein she was so deeply interested, Sandford procured a fresh and lively horse from a neighbouring yeoman, and despatched Morton with a scroll from the Prince, which gave full particulars of the battles that restored the King's authority. It also spoke of the important part our hero took in these proceedings, and of the honours that had been conferred upon him. By this means the document reached Her Majesty's hands about an hour before Savoy and his train arrived at the old palace.

After a lengthened audience with the Queen, the poor old lord was bewildered with a complication of thought that almost overpowered his senses. The energy with which the Queen advocated Sandford's claims, a circumstance so contrary to all his preconceived anticipations, the honourable position that young man had attained, the unhappy fate of De Meudon, which had been communicated by Morton, the startling results of the recent battles, were sufficient to stagger a stronger mind than Savoy's. But other considerations followed.

The youth, formerly so despised, must be innocent of all connexion with the recent outrage. The noble Lord began to think some fearful calamity had befallen the innocent, though he could hardly persuade himself of its real horror. He trembled like an aspen leaf; nor did it reassure his apprehensions when, with a want of ceremony that under ordinary circumstances would have appeared disrespectful in a person of inferior station, Kitty rushed into the apartment in a state of pallor and agitation.

" I am in no humour to hear excuses," said

Savoy, in a manner that caused the little maid to draw back and look abashed. "Your mother has wilfully deceived me; and I desire to know for what purpose háve you followed my train? By the faith of my fathers, this world is made up of mysteries."

"My Lord will not be angry," answered Kitty; "I am not come to explain my mother's absence; nor could I do so, however much my Lord may be displeased; but may I speak what is known about it?"

"I am willing to listen, provided you are truthful," said Savoy; "but it must be done briefly. I am oppressed with so many thoughts, that your mother's conduct had almost passed from my memory."

"Then I will endeavour not to weary my Lord," said Kitty. "I left my mother at Seaford, and saw her depart over the wild downs to obey my Lord's commands. In childish folly, I conceived a plan to follow my mother to Guildford, hoping to obtain service."

Here Kitty blushed deeply, knowing she was slightly perverting the truth.

" Well, go on," said Savoy, encouragingly.

" I then walked to Fletching wood, and watched the approach of my Lord's train," continued Kitty; " but not finding my mother, I followed so far, that at last I was frightened to return."

" And am I to understand that you know nothing further of your mother's proceedings?" said Savoy.

" Nothing, my Lord," said Kitty; " my mother must have lost herself on those wild hills. The night was dark, and, there wandering, I anticipate she failed to reach the Castle before daylight."

" I trust it may prove so," answered Savoy;

" though it would seem more probable that your
mother has been overtaken by some disaster. It
shall be investigated when I return to Pevensel,
if heaven is willing to spare me. For the present
I beg you to leave me; I am weary and oppressed
by a confusion of thoughts."

" My Lord will forgive me," replied Kitty,
" but I have else to say that is even of deeper
importance. When my Lady was dragged away
in the forest, I hid myself, overcome with terror.
After some time I ventured from seclusion, and
passed the bodies of the men who fell in that
brief encounter. This little scroll I drew from
the girdle of a wretch who has met the death he
deserves; it shows, beyond doubt, that my lady
has been conveyed to the Castle at Hurstingham."

" What?" exclaimed Savoy, turning deadly
pale, and extending his quivering hand. " Then,
in the name of heaven, let me see it."

The attendants gathered round while Savoy read the document as rapidly as aged eyes could decipher its meaning. It was written by Rochfort de Vere, and gave positive orders to his officers that they should proceed direct to Hurstingham without delay, if Lady Emmeline ventured to leave the Castle, and they were fortunate enough to get possession of her person. The noble Lord dropped the paper on the floor, and, leaning his elbows on a massive oak table, he covered his face with both hands, while the men at arms gazed upon each other in blank bewilderment, and Kitty stood opposite in an attitude expressive of pensiveness and timidity.

It is scarcely possible to give more than a vague and superficial sketch of the misery that possessed this poor old man's mind. Much must be left to the imagination. It was a well-defined picture of a wounded heart brooding over its sorrows, and at last rendered susceptible of impressions to which it had been hitherto callous. It was not a grief prompted by disappointment in some childish conceptions, forgotten the moment its motive is smothered in a desire for greater things. It was a dream of many years that had passed away. A long-cherished thought associated with the happiest days of his life had vanished like smoke absorbed in boundless space. She was gone; and if in recent times she might have vexed his prejudices, if she might have thwarted his whims, yet these now lie scattered on the ground like a broken vessel. It was too late to repent, the evil had come upon his house. In fancy he could hear his old comrade, De Manville, again recounting the miseries endured by his unhappy child. And though the object on which he doted was not the natural offspring of his body, yet from earliest childhood she had been regarded as the darling object of his existence. The beauty of her innocence, in riper

years, had won his heart; and in spite of little
vexations that peculiar circumstances created, he
loved her still with a fond and devoted adoration.
The treasure was never more dear, or more ap-
preciated than in the moment it was lost.

But there are other motives for regret—a consciousness of error, a sense of injustice, a bitter
recollection of wrong to one who had been his
greatest benefactor. These were perplexities,
but not irreparable disasters. If he could ask
forgiveness, if he could make an honest and
hearty reparation, all would, doubtless, be forgotten. He could have done so, and in a manner
that would gladden many hearts had that lovely
girl still been his to bestow. But the fair opportunity was gone; and as reflection brought the
terror of recent calamities before him, little by
little, and step by step, the obstinacy of his acts
stole upon the heart-broken Lord, in spite of
a slender and unavailing resistance. There

were many precautions neglected. Prudence had
been despised in the pride of self-confidence and
haste. The most trifling foresight might have
prevented all. Here that weary spirit sunk into
abject remorse. The future offered nothing but
a dark and dreary waste, embittered with the
recollections of the past. The attendants gazed
in alarm upon the picture of oppression before
them. A belief possessed them all that the
venerable Lord had bid farewell to Pevensel for
ever. Is there none on earth who can bring
relief? or must those grey hairs bow down with
sorrow to the grave?

This interval of silence was at last disturbed by
a loud clattering of horse's hoofs. Kitty and
several of the men-at-arms rushed to the window,
attentively watching the newly-arrived troopers,
who filed through the narrow gateway in the
outer court of the palace two abreast, some three
to four hundred strong. Savoy remained still

and motionless in the same attitude, while this pick and flower of the Prince's army spread themselves round the old palace. A busy hum of voices soon followed. Each seemed endeavouring to outvie his companions in imparting the earliest news of recent events. A heavy footstep gradually approached the room where Savoy sat bewailing his loss, and with a consistent dignity of mien, Sandford advanced to meet the worthy lord, who, some six weeks since had renounced his acquaintance. The old man shrank slightly back, and then grasping the young knight's extended hand with honest fervour, he desired the attendants to withdraw. Little Kitty was the last to pass out, and she carefully closed the doors behind the retiring servants, leaving age and youth alone together.

After Morton delivered the despatch with which Sandford entrusted him, he soon got into conversation with some of Savoy's retainers, and gleaned all particulars concerning the noble lord's arrival, and of Lady Emmeline's disaster. The latter circumstance awakened the utmost interest in his mind, though he had no acquaintance with the fair sufferer beyond hearsay. Without a moment's delay, the young husband mounted a swift steed, intending to retrace his steps for the purpose of meeting Sandford, and imparting early intelligence of this startling occurrence. But shortly after leaving the town he arrived at the junction of two roads, and in thoughtless haste selected the wrong one. Onward he rode for several miles, until he traversed a longer distance than would have reached the desired halting place, before he discovered his error. On this emergency he turned the horse's head, and re-entered the town of Guildford in time to gain a partial glimpse of the horsemen arriving at the old palace.

When Sandford alighted, he recognized one or

two familiar faces often seen at Pevensel, and consequently he concluded Savoy must have already arrived, as the Prince anticipated. And although he had been haunted by uncomfortable apprehensions, he very naturally imagined that Lady Emmeline was also the Queen's guest. This latter circumstance may account for the impatience with which he entered the building, and on passing the apartment where Savoy was seated, he caught sight of the noble lord in the attitude already described, and struck with his dejected appearance, though in entire ignorance as to its cause, he threw off all hesitation, and determined to try and administer some consolation, be the sorrow what it might, even at the risk of encountering a repulse.

"Young man," began Savoy, in a voice that faltered with emotion, "accept the expression of my deep pleasure at the distinction you have so honourably earnt. The joy of my life is gone,

and a calamity has fallen upon my old age, that
I can scarce find voice to speak."

" Is it in my power to offer any comfort to
your sorrows?" replied Sandford, " or am I
directly or indirectly its unhappy cause? I trust
that no irreparable misfortune has befallen you?"

" My heart is oppressed with many recollections," answered Savoy. " Any wrong sustained
at my hands I implore you to forget. There is
no request you can now make I would not grant."

" And there is but one I would ask," returned
Sandford.

" Which I can easily anticipate," said Savoy.
" The Queen has already received my consent to
your wishes, and I beg you not to ask the motive
that has induced me to give it, but the past must
all be buried in oblivion."

" It is already so in my mind," rejoined Sandford. " Let us not waste time in worthless recri-
minations. What is your present trouble? Has

your niece suffered any disaster? Do not withhold the truth a moment, everything may depend
on immediate action."

"Fearful as they are, I will tell you the correct
facts," said Savoy. "To my deep sorrow I
forced my niece to leave Pevensel against her
will. Upbraid me not, this aged heart is swollen
with unbearable grief. When two miles from
this place, a band of warriors suddenly broke
my train, and carried away the beloved girl. My
retainers did their best, and several were slain.
This scroll, found by Portevin's daughter, revealed
the sad truth; my child, for such I ever esteem
her, is conveyed to Hurstingham. Save her, I
implore you. I am old and feeble—she is yours
—I here commend her to your care. Bring her
to me again in safety and honour, and my head
shall never lay down to rest without blessing
your worthy name."

"I much dread the unhappy lady may sink from terror," said Sandford, after a short pause of bewilderment. "There is some good foundation for hope. To my certain knowledge, Rochfort de Vere cannot be at Hurstingham; he is shut up in the Castle at Kenilworth, where I left Conisburgh with a powerful force to intercept him, should any attempt be made at escape."

"Oh! merciful Heaven, this is joyful intelligence!" exclaimed Savoy. "Were you present when De Meudon fell, and was it by Rochfort himself he was slain?"

"No," answered Sandford, "he rushed on too impetuously, and was surrounded by men-at-arms. Though unhappily too late, I hastened to the rescue with a number of men, or De Vere would have become my prisoner. But we have no time to talk of the dead, however worthy they may be."

"He was the son of a noble sire," replied

Savoy. "His loss alone would give me a bitter sorrow if nothing else oppressed my soul."

"Let us silently sip a cup of wine to his memory," said Sandford, "and in haste, for I must hence away. There is another surprise awaiting you. The domains at Hurstingham are attainted from De Vere and conferred upon myself. By some means I will make my way into the Castle, and hold it against him should he elude the vigilance of Conisburgh or remain in his hiding place."

"I rejoice at it," said Savoy. "You are aware it was taken from De Meudon's father to be given to that detested knight, De Vere. I may live long enough to see my old friend's wrong avenged."

"But one brief word more," replied Sandford. "Do you remain here, or return to Pevensel? If the latter, I have something that may interest you, which can be retained or destroyed, as may seem most discreet."

" My bodily ailments need rest and quietude," said Savoy. " I shall return to Pevensel on the morrow. What is this new mystery?"

" It is the attainder on your domains. I found it left in Rochfort de Vere's tent," replied Sandford.

" Your services deserve more than my power can bestow. Would to Heaven that dear girl was here that I might place her hand in your's and pronounce a blessing upon both !"

" Fear not," rejoined Sandford, " you shall do so within the old walls of Pevensel, if Heaven is pleased to sustain your niece's strength under such apprehension. There shall we meet again. In safety and honour, I fondly trust, to restore the joys of your life, and then claim the prize as my own."

Savoy was about to reply in a hearty affirmative, but the young man was gone. Still a picture of age is left, indulging its fancied longings like a child. It is difficult to utterly eradicate a fixed idea, even by the plainest exhibition of consequences. All the noble lord's former pride would have returned as danger receded, had the motive for it still existed. He would have given a preference to De Meudon as a man of higher rank, but this cherished imagination was no longer possible. Even the arguments of the Queen prevailed nothing until he was informed of that young valiant's end. He had been forced into concession by necessity rather than choice. The very chance of his apprehensions being relieved flattered many old infirmities. But let us be charitable to his aged and harrowed soul, let him retire to rest and prepare for the journey on the morrow, with his slumbers let all vanities sleep also. Old man, pomp and grandeur still are thine, though the pride of genius may be kinsman to your noble house.

When Sandford quitted the noble lord's presence, the first who accosted him was little Kitty. He listened briefly to the history of her missing mother, and any particulars she could give concerning the outrage on Lady Emmeline. For the present he admonished her to remain at Guildford, where he expected Conisburgh would probably arrive on the following day, as that good man was instructed to leave his post when the King's forces arrived at the Castle at Kenilworth. He told her to desire the faithful servant to follow him with all speed to Hurstingham; and after giving the little maid a sum of money to provide any immediate needs, he added that whatever might be her mother's fate, she would always find a friend in him for her poor father's sake. With this assurance the little maid skipped gaily away and took up a lodging with the tanner who had conducted her to the town.

Upon this, a consultation followed with Morton and some officers from Pevensel. Our hero desired them to collect the largest band that could be mustered at a few minutes' notice while he proceeded to have a short interview with the Queen to do that homage which her station demanded, and to deliver some further credentials which had been entrusted to his care. He was cheerfully excused at the earliest moment possible, Her Majesty dispensing with many customary ceremonies, and heartily wishing him good speed in the enterprise he was about to undertake.

On his return he found a troop of one hundred and fifty men, all ready and armed *cap-à-pie*. It is hardly needful to say that Morton was amongst them, holding a well harnessed steed beside the one he himself rode. On this animal Sandford mounted, and after waving his hand to Savoy, who stood at a window to watch the departure before he retired to rest, the word was given to march, and at a smart trot the confines of the town were soon passed.

As the troop rode through the forest dingles, our young hero did not give way to the slightest despondency. He had encountered greater difficulties and surmounted them with success. There is but one more that blocked the way to the height of his ambition. He had a conscious pride that this end had been so far attained by honourable exertion. He may have been endowed by nature with peculiar gifts and talents, superior to the average genius of a dark age, but his good fortune was mainly due to the energy with which he used these qualities. Many may work hard without producing results, either owing to want of abilities or the absence of opportunity to display any gifts they possess.

But no happy talent will compensate for the want of earnestness. The first is the root of success, the other the soil wherein it must grow.

As the gallant band proceeded on their route, many little reconnoitering parties disengaged themselves from the main body of the troopers, and without avail endeavoured to discover the hostile force that carried off the fair prize. As evening closed in the progress that had been made was by no means satisfactory to Sandford, though he was compelled to make many allowances for the delay. The steeds were mostly wearied after a long morning journey, and the men unacquainted with the country. When about three miles from Hurstingham, the worthy commander selected two retainers, who were mounted on light and fresh palfreys obtained at Guildford, and desired them to ride forward with Morton, hoping to ascertain whether the unhappy maiden had yet reached her destination. After breaking the cover of the forest, the three advance guards ascended a mound about half-a-mile from the Castle. Here they espied the hostile cavalcade crossing the drawbridge, and watched them until the closing gate hid the last man from their view.

CHAPTER X.

" Dreams in their development have breath,
   And tears, and tortures, and the touch of joy;
   They leave a weight upon our waking thoughts,
   They make us what we are not, what they will,
   And shake us with the vision that's gone by."
                                          BYRON.

ON arriving at Hurstingham, Lady Emmeline
and her attendant were ushered into an apartment of rude and dreary aspect. It contained no
article of furniture beyond an old couch, and was
ill-suited to so distinguished a captive. A small
opening at the top admitted light and air, and

these great disadvantages were only compensated
for by the privacy it afforded. It is probable
that the principal guest chambers had fallen into
great decay from long neglect and ill-usage, and
consequently the officers in charge selected this
gloomy cell as the best accommodation it was in
their power to afford.

When the door had closed upon her, Lady
Emmeline sat down upon the couch, and gazed
round the apartment with a lost and vacant expression. She was for a time deprived of all
power of utterance. Her wide-opened eyes were
red with blood-shot veins, and, tossing her arms
wildly, she tore down her auburn locks, which
streamed carelessly to her waist. A flood of
tears would have afforded a welcome relief, but
the source of sorrow's fountain was dried up,
parched with the very excess of grief and despair.
Anne seated herself beside her mistress, placed
an arm round her shoulders, and looked into her

lovely but altered countenance, while a darkening night gradually threw its solemn blackness around. The silver moonbeams had forced their way through the unclosed opening, and shed a pale lustre upon the two figures, before any words were exchanged.

" Can you not speak to me, my dear mistress?" said Anne. " There is a good hope left yet ; be calm and trustful."

" Speak not of it," said Emmeline, wildly, and after a long pause. " Hope in what? Hope in infamy and disgrace ? No, it is not on earth. There may be in heaven, and only there to those who are utterly lost. Why have you brought me here ?—you, I say—go—and leave me ; I can die alone."

" It is only your faithful Anne that is beside you," said the domestic. " I will never leave you. Oh ! think, my dear mistress, under what great terrors heaven has sustained you. It will not withhold its care, in this, the deepest of all."

"It is that I am a sinner, a base and worthless sinner," cried Emmeline, endeavouring to disengage herself from Anne's grasp. "Have these worthless wretches bribed you to keep me here? I have been disobedient—have broken a solemn promise. He will not forgive—oh! never; he will leave me now, despise me, laugh at me in this torture."

"My dear mistress, who will laugh at you?" said Anne, while feeling her brow, that burnt like a furnace. "No good friend will forsake you that never wronged any one on earth; endeavour now to sleep, it will refresh your heated brain."

"There is no sleep but the one long one," replied Emmeline; "no repose but the grave. Oh! it would be a welcome moment, a joy, for which my prayers are earnest. Oh! forgive me; I forgot you, my good and faithful girl."

" Be not afraid, there is another near; a God that watches over the weak," said Anne. "He has before raised a strong arm to your succour. Come, recline upon this couch. I will not leave your side. Try and sleep; to-morrow may bring us help."

At this moment Anne succeeded in persuading her mistress to recline upon the rude bed, and she sunk into a stupor, never offering a reply when called by name, nor did a gesture follow the mention of one adored youth, a word most likely to produce a response. The servant then contented herself with a patient watchfulness. It was a depressive exhaustion, succeeding a condition of unhappy excitement. Come, weariness, perform a welcome work. She sleeps; it is a sleep of maiden purity, though the brain is still perturbed with visionary imaginations. A dazzling ray of light broke from the cloudless sky. The whole canopy of heaven burst into a vivid glare, like a sea of adamant. In transparent loveliness a bright angel descended, supported by thin and curly vapours. The massive gate of the Castle swung back before the approaching spectre. It stands in that narrow cell, and gazes upon sleep, calm in the beauty of holiness, clothed in celestial shape, it is still a well-known form, calling to remembrance the happy days of childhood. It is Marion, whose noble father sunk to rest on the field at Lewes. It is silent and motionless. Oh! speak, if only to repeat those words of childish mirth uttered in playful hours of infancy. They would soften the passing moments of earthly misery. No sound escaped its rosy lips. An uplifted arm points to a coming vision, which gradually approached in mortal and more questionable shape. A noble youth stands surrounded by a host of mighty warriors. It is he. The one on whose fortunes heaven has bestowed its smiles. Another fairy spirit descended from above, and placed a victor's wreath upon that manly brow. The spirit whispers in his ear, pointing towards that massive Castle, where beauty steals a placid moment from bitter anguish. Then with rapid wing it flies back to the gorgeous mansions from whence it came.

The maiden starts erect upon the couch, but the ideal has vanished before the reality. All is darkness, and the faithful servant supports her trembling form.

"Oh! would he not come to me? Have I so wronged him that he consigns me to perdition? Anne, did you not speak?"

"There is no one here, my dear mistress," said the servant.

"Then it is a dream, a happy transient dream," answered Emmeline, "that only enhances the horror of my wakeful hours. Forgive me."

"You know me now, dear mistress," replied

Anne. "I have never ceased to watch. That light sleep has composed your thoughts. Believe me, these troubles are as painful to my bosom as thine; but I am hopeful. There is no lord of the Castle within these walls, and this evil may turn to good."

"Anne, you are ten times better than I am, and more unassuming in your goodness," said Emmeline, her mind now calm after the repose of sleep. "I will try to be hopeful, and put a faithful trust in heaven, even in this extremity of danger. Calamity often exalts our strength, shows us the evil of our nature, its weakness, and want of some great sustaining power on high. For your sake I will not despair, and if the worst fate awaits me, I have a happy consciousness it is not deserved."

"Then endeavour to think so," said Anne, "and recline once more to sleep. It is a long and dreary night. But my lady should know better than I can what is right, what thoughtful care God shows to those who trust in him. I am but a poor ignorant girl, while my lady is learned. If to my ignorant mind the way to consolation is open, it must be clearer to those who better understand its mysteries."

" You are a good creature," answered Emmeline, leaning on her domestic's bosom, while the first tear forced itself down her cheeks. " Oh ! my beloved uncle, what must be his thoughts. And years steal upon him, and already his form totters under their weight of care. If I die within these walls, and you are permitted to meet him once more, convey my last blessing, and say that in my last words I forgave all the past."

" He is old and feeble," said Anne ; " and we must make allowance for his infirmities, both of mind and body. His impaired strength can give very little aid, but there is one young and vigorous who will soon fly to my lady's help, when he knows her danger."

"It is a forlorn hope," answered Emmeline. " Ere this he may have perished in some fearful battle, or be engaged in some mighty enterprise, too great to be neglected for one weak and foolish girl ; besides my fate would be sealed before he could be aware of it, and these iron gates would be closed upon him."

" Nay, try and believe it yet," said Anne; " he knew of my lady's danger when Pevensel was besieged. Though far away, he found a way into that Castle while surrounded by hostile foes, and brought my lady the succour she needed."

"Yes, Anne," replied Emmeline; "I know all, and am deeply grateful for his care. But he will never dream of this calamity, when I promised so faithfully not to leave Pevensel. It is my own folly and imprudence that brings this bitter punishment."

" Say not so, my lady," answered Anne. " It was in obedience to your uncle's command, which you could not longer resist without provoking greater disaster."

" We must try and forget that," said Emmeline. " God forbid I should utter one word of recrimination against his grey hairs, his anger has died away, and bitterness of sorrow will bring him to a cold grave."

" It is an unhappy result," returned Anne ; " though the worst is not come, and a good Providence may avert it. I implore my lady to sleep once more upon this rough bed. To-morrow may bring some bright joy, that will contrast strangely with the terror of this dark night."

" I could endure this patiently, even for a

week, if Heaven is only pleased to avert any greater calamity," replied Emmeline. "But my head is light and weak, and delirium will again seize me if I continue to talk; leave me not, and let us both breathe a silent prayer."

"Commit yourself to my care, dear mistress," said Anne; "even if the worst is to happen, determination is often a safeguard. The strongest men are cowards when conscious of evil acts, and strength is often given from above, equal to any emergency, however desperate. Now sleep calmly."

"I trust to you and Heaven," said Emmeline. "Good night, sweet angels protect us. Thank Heaven my reason is still spared."

The first sunbeam of the morn fell through a narrow opening upon a holy sleep. Its early moments were disturbed with convulsive starts,

while fancy's vision passed through the maiden's
breast with sudden and frantic imaginations.
But exhaustion was too great, they failed to
break the peaceful slumber of innocence. The
trace of terror and care gradually vanish; how
peaceful, how divinely pure that happy face,
when sorrow and fear is absorbed in the alluring
grace of beauteous repose; some happy thought
engages the mind in a light dream. Is it that
happy thought which, of all others, could bring
comfort? If so, may Heaven prolong that
slumber of loveliness until it is realized. May a
just retribution come upon the evil conceived
against that placid sleeper, and unlooked for
protection shelter maidenhood in its purity.

The gaudy radiance of noon is come. It finds
the peaceful maiden still calm in that happy
sleep. The faithful domestic had not quitted her
side, nor had she once removed her eye from that

beauteous face since daylight broke into the little cell. A loud tramp of heavy footsteps suddenly echoed through the distant corridors. It is not heard by that guileless sleeper. Anne stepped lightly to the door, and with one finger erect, pointing upward, she stood in an attitude of listening contemplation, as a busy hum of voices fell upon her ear. But it is in vain. Those murmuring syllables are unintelligible, and fail to reach the confines of that narrow chamber.

Leaving Anne still endeavouring to decipher these mysterious sounds, and the fair lady to enjoy her slumbers, our steps must be retraced to the mound where Morton and his companions saw the cavalcade enter the Castle. They at once returned to Sandford, to communicate this intelligence, and the new Knight commanded the troop to halt and partake of refreshment, while he endeavoured to devise some means for the lady's relief.

The Castle before him was now his own, though it was improbable that the officers in charge would open the gates in obedience to his commands. The force that accompanied him was unprovided with means for an assault, and such a measure might only provoke immediate violence to the unhappy captives. So our young hero decided to place a strong guard upon the only approach by which the Castle could be reached, and to await patiently for intelligence of Conisburgh's proceedings. In this determination he waited until night closed in, and then approaching stealthily, took up a strong position at the commencement of the long vista of fir trees that led to the drawbridge of the fortress.

It was a frequent theme of Sandford's thoughts during that night, whether by bribes or some

other means, a communication might be sent to
Lady Emmeline, that would soften the virulence
of her apprehensions. But the more he reflected
on this subject, the more he felt satisfied that
such an attempt was neither prudent nor desirable.
He rejoiced that the faithful Anne had crossed
the drawbridge beside her mistress, for Morton's
long-sighted vision had distinguished two female
figures alone in the centre of the cavalcade ; and
invoking the care of heaven upon the maiden's
fears, he was more than ever convinced that information of hostile forces threatening the castle
would be prejudicial to ultimate success.

In the calmness of night a vision of former
days passed through his mind. Considering the
temper and spirit of the times, and considering
also the pride and haughtiness of Savoy, he was
almost amazed to think how such an idea as
alliance with the distinguished lady, now within

the massive walls before him, could ever have possessed his mind. But so it did. It was a fancy of youth, that grew into an ambition of manhood; and as he looked upon the future, his ideas seemed to snatch a glimpse of a coming life, as the eye would rest upon a beautiful garden graced with the loveliness of nature's gaudy flowers. It appeared to this child of fortune that youthful imaginations are not so visionary as many are apt to consider them, but that in the apparent impossibility of early fancies, the germ of manly energies are often sown, to rise to a lofty and wide-spreading tree, in years of matured discretion.

When daylight again dawned upon the re-freshed warriors, Sandford dispatched a small detachment to a neighbouring village to procure eatables. Another party hunted in the forest. By this means an ample repast was prepared before noon, and after thoroughly satisfying the inner man, the troopers arranged themselves in small groups to quaff cups for the success of the undertaking on which they were engaged. While these stimulating draughts animated their spirits, a hoarse trumpet blew far and shrill from a distant mound. All flew to arms, and looked upon the sunlit hillock. A small knot of horsemen waved a banner in triumphant exultation, and then descending from the commanding eminence, they approached the avenue of firs at a rapid gallop.

CHAPTER XI.

"There is no strange handwriting on the wall,
 Thro' all the midnight hum no threatening call,
 Nor on the marble floor the stealthy fall
 Of fatal footsteps ; all is safe, thou fool,
 The avenging deities are shod with wool."

W. A. BUTLER.

IN point of time, our narrative must retrogade a
few days, and the imagination be carried back to
the forest near Kenilworth, at the moment when
the poor woman Margot was being carried to her
peaceful grave, and Conisburgh was narrowly

watching the busy movement at the gate of the Castle.

Shortly after the battle of Evesham, the King despatched a messenger to desire the surrender of Kenilworth Castle, then held by De Mountfort the younger. This command being met with a flat and positive denial, the officer at once departed, after openly informing the garrison that the King's army would immediately attack their stronghold, and he did not forget to communicate to Rochfort de Vere the intelligence of the forfeiture of his domain at Hurstingham, and its gift to Sandford.

Without waiting to contemplate the ungovernable fit of passion to which that despoiled knight gave way, it will be more to the purpose of our narrative to picture his rage cooled down after the first outburst, and to dwell upon the conclusions these circumstances produced in his mind.

He was satisfied that in a few days the King's forces would draw a strong cordon round the stronghold where he had found a temporary refuge, and there he would be confined for several weeks, with the probability of ultimately becoming a prisoner. Meanwhile he had no doubt Sandford would take measures to possess himself of Hurstingham, and hold it against him. Much as he detested that young man, he had experienced sufficient of his energies to forbid even a momentary imagination that any time or opportunity would be lost. Influenced by these fears he determined to leave Kenilworth with ten followers. He would endeavour to reach Hurstingham at all risks, and if fortunate enough to gain the shelter of its walls, he would defy his deadly foe until the last extremity.

So closely had Conisburgh and his band concealed themselves that De Vere did not believe any danger would arise in the neighbourhood of the stronghold he was about to quit. But as he crossed the turfy sward, which spread its soft carpet between the Castle and the forest, a vigilant eye soon recognised the device on his gaudy banner, and the well-known drab surcoat that encircled his massive form.

" My turn is now come," thought the man who stood on the verge of the forest. " How many comrades have I seen tortured to death to satisfy the brutality of that detested fiend! How often has my back smarted under the undeserved lash to please his savage whims! Beware! for vengeance now approaches with noiseless steps."

The alarm was soon raised, and Conisburgh placed his men in a convenient position to intercept the coming horsemen immediately they penetrated the wood. The ten followers are surrounded, dragged from their horses, and made

prisoners before they had time to offer resistance ;
while Rochfort de Vere broke away from his
antagonists. He dashed swiftly through the
forest, closely followed by Conisburgh and
about thirty men, who were provided with
horses.

Without gaining upon the fugitive knight, the
pursuers managed to keep their ground, and
never once lost sight of the prey. Flying onward
still, the chase is kept up with vigour, until a
bend of the river Avon interrupted the progress
of the steeds. The hot blood rose to De Vere's
eyes. Was he to surrender to a man formerly his
slave? No; he would dare anything before sub-
mitting to such humiliation. And galloping onward towards the broad stream he discovered a
rude bridge constructed of planks, though only
of sufficient substance to carry foot passengers.
It was worth the venture. Once across that frail

structure his foes could only follow one by one, if they even had the courage to attempt the passage. He could then cope with them single-handed.

With a courage that desperation could only have imparted, De Vere dashed upon the wooden stage, and the horse, terrified at the sound of the rushing waters, turned restive and unmanageable. The frantic animal trod upon a rotten plank at the verge of the structure. The decayed board immediately parted in the centre. The steed was thrown upon its side, and, still carrying its dismayed rider, both fell into the deep waters beneath with a booming splash. Encumbered with heavy trappings the steed went down; its legs became entangled in the stiff withies that bowed before the flowing element, and the rider's foot was locked in the stirrup. Both sunk to rise no more. Conisburgh and his companions stood on the brink of the river for two hours, but no visible evidence of the late occurrence presented itself, save the broken fragments of the shattered bridge; while the stream murmured gently on through the placid vales, unsullied by the pollution it had engulphed.

So perished this cruel and evil man. Despised by the strong, a tool in the hands of his betters, he was the oppressor of the weak, the terror of the needy and forlorn. But his dreams of guilt are passed;—no more unhappy serfs would be the victims of his passion, no more tender maidens pine under the brutality of his licentious acts; and, happily, the remembrance of these evil deeds will fade away, while his carcase rots in its watery grave.

Although he could not smother an inward satisfaction, it must be recorded to Conisburgh's credit that he never indulged in triumphant exultations when his former master perished.

But duly satisfied that all was at an end, he returned to the men left in charge of the captives, who all recognised him as an old comrade. He immediately addressed them in the following language :—

" My old comrades, your tyrannical master is no more; swear allegiance to the brave knight in whose service I am now engaged. You will have no cause to regret the act, and can procure an immediate release.from bondage."

A hearty response followed this proposition, All swore fidelity to a new master, and not one amongst them did so with a sentiment of regret. This concluded, Conisburgh collected a band of twenty followers, including the two principal officers from the new reinforcement, and, leaving the others to follow at their own. leisure, he dashed across the country towards the town of Guildford, only halting at night for necessary rest. He also carried with him the banner of the deceased knight as a trophy of his achievements.

It was on the morning after Sandford departed for the Castle at Hurstingham that Kitty Portevin was seen seated upon a stone at the outskirts of the town of Guildford, watching anxiously for any sign of approaching travellers. Her patience was not tried beyond two hours, when a small band of horsemen arrived, and the leader, after eyeing her in vacant astonishment for a few moments, commanded a halt, and, dismounting from his steed, ran towards the little maid, whom he had not seen since her father's death, and, catching her tenderly in his arms, he implanted several fervent kisses upon a pair of ruddy cheeks.

Before Conisburgh had time to make any inquiries, Kitty briefly recounted the whole his-

tory of her adventure since her father's death, the
mystery concerning her mother, the capture of
Lady Emmeline, and her interview with Sandford.   The young man on his part exulted in the
revenge exacted for the old seaman.   Revenge
executed upon the Knight, for whose behalf the
murder was perpetrated, and it had been ascertained beyond doubt that the officer who contrived the wicked plot was slain at Kenilworth.
He had great fears that Rosanne Portevin was
lost, and finding the little maid greatly distressed
by his apprehensions, he seated her on a sloping
bank, and placing his arm round her waist, he
endeavoured to cheer her spirits, while the men
digressed from the main road for a short distance,
and refreshed their animals from the cool waters
of a limpid pool.   The young servant did not
forget his promises, he had engaged to be the
protector of that little maid, and her desolate

condition of orphanage and destitution added greatly to the warmth of his affection.

"I will not deceive you, or promise what is impossible," said Conisburgh; "if your mother is lost, trust to me as a faithful protector. I have wealth, and the strength to make good use of it."

"And from whence did this wealth come?" answered Kitty; "I understood your fortunes were bound up with another's?"

"So they are," replied Conisburgh, "and one on whom fortune has showered its smiles. But have you not heard your father mention an old woman named Margot?"

"Often," said Kitty, "is she now alive? It is believed she had treasure hidden up, which my father anticipated would be mine after his son perished, but the old thing took a whim into her head that no woman must inherit it."

"And do you know for why?" said Conisburgh.

"Something about the stars that shone at her son's birth," answered Kitty. "Is she dead or living?"

"She is dead," replied Conisburgh; "the treasure is mine, and not mine alone, there is another to share it. Kitty, dearest, it shall be equally yours. So try to forget your troubles; be the little sprightly maid that won the heart of all your father's friends, and let us live for each other."

"I will endeavour to do so," answered Kitty; "yet how sorely must I try your patience. I have no guardian but my mother, and if she is dead, then none save my uncle, who has left for Spain."

"But we will not assume your mother dead," returned Conisburgh. "Wait until the fair lady is released at Hurstingham, then I shall be returning to Pevensel, and will search the country round if she is still missing."

"And should you find her it will not help us," said Kitty. "My mother is prejudiced against everyone, she will not hear a word."

"You mistake," replied Conisburgh; "she was rich, I a poor dependant. Now she is in want, and my coffers full of silver. Those words will sound like sweet music. Fear it not, and in need we can only wait your uncle's return. If it is for seven years I will be faithful, nor shall my heart incline to others."

"It shall be as you desire," said Kitty. "My uncle will return in two years, if heaven is willing to preserve him from the dangers of the seas; until then, where can I remain?"

"Trouble not to think of that," replied Conisburgh. "I will find many good friends who will give you shelter and protection. And why should we despair? Some of the treasure stolen after your father's death may be recovered; so be of good cheer; now let us away to Hurstingham, and if you have confidence in me—"

"I will trust you to convey me anywhere," answered Kitty. "It is my pride to be deemed worthy of your notice and approbation."

"And it is my pleasure to dwell in your little heart," returned Conisburgh. "Come, we must not lose time, the men are impatient; first, then, to Guildford, and the midday sun shall find us at Hurstingham."

Remounted on a strong charger, with Kitty seated on the saddle before him, Conisburgh arrived at Guildford in time to witness Savoy's departure on the return to Pevensel. But it was impossible to trifle long with that hard master—Time. The noble lord was obliged to content himself with a hurried account of Rochfort's death, and, after bestowing a good reward, he bid the young man speed away to Hurstingham. The poor old man is wending his course back. He had tasted the cup of bitterness, and though the excitement had seriously weakened his already shattered frame, he regarded the rest of his life as time spared to atone for the past.

Having procured fresh horses, the journey to Hurstingham was accomplished with extraordinary rapidity. On reaching the mound, the trumpet sounded as described in our last chapter, then waving the banner taken from the deceased knight, the little band soon became mingled with the troopers awaiting outside the castle. With bursting eagerness, Conisburgh communicated the intelligence which need not be recapitulated. The news produced a loud and hearty cheer, that aroused the men within the stronghold, who soon lined the ramparts, when the two prisoners, that swore allegiance to a new master, advanced with the banner, and making a signal to the garrison, the drawbridge was lowered, and Sandford, with all his train, passed the massive gate. Here arose the busy hum of voices, to which Anne is still listening. Here the remainder of the servants bound themselves in oath of fidelity to the new lord of the domain, and so accustomed had they been to endure a weight of arrogance, that all stared in vacant surprise, as Sandford shook each one cordially by the hand.

From that eventful day a new existence dawned upon our young hero. He was to be envied, and not despised. He had thrown the whole energies of his life on one object, and it was attained. But he often thought how easily it might have been far otherwise. How long had he been sailing on the waters of chance before his bark was safely to port! He thought of many who had tried the passage of that ruffled sea, so beset with rocks and rolling quicksands, and, mistaken in their soundings, had foundered in its depth. Here, at the summit of his success, Sandford's reason was about to forsake him. He would have rushed to the apartment where Lady Emmeline slumbered with the wildest ecstasy. The first moment of success is rarely the most dignified in a man's life.

It was here that a little maid shewed the greater discretion; Kitty suggested that the terror under which Lady Emmeline must have been suffering would lead to over excitement on so sudden a change of circumstances, and Sandford at once perceiving the wisdom of her arguments, desired her to go and inform the faithful Anne of his presence, and caution her to break it gently to her mistress. The little orphan skipped down the corridor, and tapped gently at the door, where Anne still stood in her listening posture; and speaking in a low voice that was soon recognized, she beckoned the faithful domestic from the chamber, who, advancing cautiously, was accosted by Sandford. The young knight desired her to wait until her lady awoke, and then to acquaint the happy sleeper with her altered fate. Unconsciously she is sleeping still, no longer the captive of a brutal fiend, but the guest of an adored youth, beloved as a past deliverer, a present helper, and a future protector.

When that weary maiden sunk to sleep it was in the darkness of a dreary night. Her fate, her terrors, all seemed as black as the gloominess that surrounded her couch. But when the moment of wakefulness arrived, the noonday sun shone in all its gaudy radiance. Her future was joy, bright as the vivid ray which pierced the retirement of that little cell. She knew it not. The sounds of joy and exultation now reached her chamber. Were they to mock her in misery and despair? No; the faithful Anne told the tale, not in words, but a face beamed with smiles. There was freedom from care and anxiety depicted upon her countenance.

"What is it?" said Emmeline, "can a pleasing thought possess you even in this fearful place?"

"My lady is safe," answered Anne; "the old lord of this Castle is dead, and his body lies twenty feet beneath the surface of the waters."

"Merciful heaven!" answered Emmeline. "May his sins meet a pardon that was impossible on earth! How did you gain this intelligence?"

"Oh! my lady," replied Anne, "the world is completely changed. The Prince has gained a victory, and the Earl is slain; this Castle is con-

ferred upon a new lord who has arrived to claim
his possessions."

" Can these things be?" answered Emmeline.
" Oh, heaven! I cannot express my thankfulness.
But can I rely on the new lord's protection?"

" He is a worthy young Knight," returned
Anne, " in whom my lady will have the deepest
confidence.   " Nor could this domain have been
conferred on one more entitled to such a gift.
Perhaps my lady could form some guess."

" You cannot mean the young knight from
whose father the Castle was originally taken?"
said Emmeline.

" No, my lady," said Anne; " that good youth
is laid in the Church of St. Nicholas, at Kenilworth.   He fell nobly, and peace be to his
soul!"

" Oh! Anne, you chill every drop of blood in
my veins," answered Emmeline.   "I remember

him in earlier childhood within these walls; but who, then, is the lord of this Castle? I implore you to tell me."

At this moment the door opened, and, unable to endure any further suspense, Sandford stepped into the chamber. The truth was at once revealed.

The lady darted from the couch, clasped her deliverer frantically round the neck, exclaiming—

" I am indeed saved! Do you forgive me for leaving Pevensel? and why have you come here?"

" I have come to claim my new domain," said Sandford, soothingly, " and to receive you as the first guest who has honoured me by partaking of its hospitality. I will not attempt to tell you all that has recently passed. Such excitement would weary you. Sufficient that this Castle is mine, with suitable honours, but I have greater riches in store."

" What will my uncle think of this ? " cried

Emmeline. " Can he be aware of it ? Surely he might now give some heed to our wishes."

" I have seen him at Guildford ; he knows all," answered Sandford. " Such a change of circumstances he could not resist. Dearest, you are mine."

" What !" exclaimed Emmeline. " Have you really his consent ?"

" I have his positive and solemn word," answered Sandford. " You must rest here a day or two after this excitement, then we shall depart for Pevensel to receive your uncle's blessing. He returns there this day—now forget all that is past. Let us study your poor guardian in his declining days. He would have sunk into the grave with sorrow had I not arrived to calm his fears."

" Then let us go to-morrow," said Emmeline ; once more within the old walls of Pevensel, how all my happy days will be called to remembrance. But life cannot pass without a few dark shadows.

Mine fade before the brighter scenes of happier years to come."

"It seems we are not to be perplexed at one blast of misfortune," answered Sandford. "With a reverse my life commenced when I became a prisoner at Dover. I looked upon that day as an unhappy one, thinking at the first sight that all was lost."

"Let us endeavour to think that all has been for good," replied Emmeline. "I have learnt to value your protection, and to be thankful for the care exercised over me. My life is yours, my smiles shall greet your joys, my comfort sympathise in your sorrows. So shall our days pass away."

"I will endeavour to render it so," said Sandford. "Now I leave you to rest, for it is greatly needed if to-morrow's sun is to light our road to Pevensel. For the present adieu, sweet angels protect your bed, and grant a peaceful slumber. All is safe around, dream sweetly of happy days."

It was some time before Emmeline could feel fully persuaded that she had not been possessed by some romantic dream. In thankfulness she poured forth a tribute of praise, but her mental peace was not unmingled with sorrow. She thought of that good youth now laid to rest, through the indulgence of wild enthusiasm. She shuddered to reflect upon the career of that Knight who had been her terror, and when she reviewed the craftiness with which he had endeavoured to accomplish her destruction, she thanked Heaven that her affections had earned the care of one gifted with a well-regulated judgment, who, under the guidance of some guardian spirit, had preserved her from all these dangers.

During the remainder of the day, great bustle

and activity prevailed in the Castle. Sandford
was giving numerous directions for the removal
of certain objectionable evidences of former
cruelties perpetrated within its walls. Every preparation being made, the cavalcade was to be
ready at daybreak. Morton was left as chief
officer in the Knight's absence, and shortly afterwards he was joined by his good little wife. But
he only filled this post for a few months, when
receiving some high appointment in the King's
service at Winchester, he was succeeded by the
faithful Conisburgh. As the sun sunk to its
rest, all was ready for the morrow, and the happy
maiden sleeps peacefully in that Castle, where, as
the spouse of its newly created lord, she was
destined to receive many noble and distinguished
guests in future days.

CHAPTER XII.

"She is mine own,
And I as rich in having such a jewel
As twenty seas, if all their sands were pearls,
The water nectar, and the rocks pure gold."
SHAKESPEARE.

THE morning rays beamed gaily on the lofty towers of Hurstingham on the following day. And as the eye pierced the lonely glen, which widened from the hill whereon the Castle reared its head, all breathed the same wild spirit of poetical voluptuousness. There was the pensive loveliness of the surrounding foliage, the glaring

sparkle of the distant stream, that led the contemplative mind from charm to charm, and from
beauty to beauty. It seemed a region set apart by
nature from the rest of creation, as a painting of
the romantic and picturesque.

Such was the gaudy day on which Lady
Emmeline passed out of the Castle. How
different the look cast back upon its towering
walls, to the contemplation with which she
entered them. But why should sorrow fling a
shadow on that lovely brow? Time is but short.
Why should it be a lasting scene of gloom?
Youth's blossom may be frail, and the flower of
beauty will soon fade. But where the pleasure
of summer without the smile of the rosebud, or
the sweetness of spring without the modest
violet? Where the joys of hope without the
gaiety of youth? Despoil life of its early pleasure,
and the minstrel may lay down and weep. Speed
on then, fair lady, both hope and beauty are

thine, and though the loveliest objects may fade in the night, all things are bright around, they seem nothing without thee.

Go, thou dismal vision of the past. The mountain's brow is crowned with gaudy flowers, the peaceful valleys are green. In these same vales the winter snows fell cold and dreary upon .the ground. It did not bid us mourn, and as it melted before the genial warmth of coming spring, the heart rejoiced with frantic gladness. So may terror haunt the mind, so may disappointment blight the hopes, yet there is a sunny day to come, when care shall vanish like the sunlit snows.

> " Be not dismayed
> If ill fortune blows with a wintry wind,
> Its blast may be sent for a purpose kind ;
> Full soon a spring will come, a summer flower,
> Then wander happy in contentment's bower.
> The winter snows preserve the hidden root,
> To yield in season due a laughing fruit,
> In gaudiness arrayed."

ANONYMOUS.

Taking a different route to that by which they came, the travellers once more visited the city of Winchester, and there, after partaking of refreshment, they are again on the road, passing the old stone where Sandford and Conisburgh appointed to meet when the lady was rescued from Dunsmore. Every object seemed to bring recollections of the past vividly to mind. But the lady was soon wearied, and was unequal to all the excitement she had recently endured. It was towards evening that the old towers of Arundel again broke the distant sky. Where a more suitable resting place? The noble lady had twice received our fair heroine, and sympathised in her sorrow. She would be the more ready to exult in her pleasures now every shadow of oppressive care had overpast. Nor was this conjecture disappointed. The two womanly hearts greet each ‸other at the massive gate, the fair hostess anticipating those words of joy that faltered on a maiden's tongue.

Each fair form had been a dreary pilgrim in the vale of sorrow. The worthy Lady of Arundel had beheld her lord a prisoner, his domains threatened, her sons hostages in the hand of a cruel foe, yet never lost heart or hope. The ungenerous blast of misfortune had only heightened her emotions of fondness. She had longed to meet a heart that could feel the warmth of her present raptures.

" Welcome to these halls once again," said the fair hostess ; " how often have I thought of that night when the Prior conducted you to Dunsmore? Since then you have often been present in my dreams, and heartily I thank God you are safe."

" Thanks, my dear kind friend," answered Emmeline. " Your troubles have not failed to reach my ears; I am quite excited with joy to find your worthy lord is here."

" Tell me, then, all you have endured since last we met," said the Lady of Arundel. " You have, indeed, a lover who esteems you better than his life. Let me hear how your uncle has been appeased, and I shall be able to rejoice the better."

In as few words as a long story could possibly be condensed, Emmeline recounted the whole history contained in these pages. Her relief from Dunsmore, the siege of Pevensel, the prejudices of her uncle; and her capture near Guildford. But, with greater fervency, she told all Sandford's adventures, his escapes, his brilliant services rendered to the Prince, and the honours and possessions he had consequently earnt. And, while the red blood tinted her cheeks, she spoke of her guardian's consent to the one object she had long held dear.

" Then, in the remembrance of these dangers incurred for your safety, you will love him the more truly," said the Lady of Arundel. " There are many rough waves to oppose us in the voyage of life, but these rude blasts only warm the inward affections of the heart."

" It will do so," answered Emmeline. " I can dote on him. He has removed all the strong impediments of my uncle's prejudice. My fond heart must ever adore, and the music of my soul speak what no uttered words can say."

" Such is true happiness," said the Lady of Arundel. " I have known days embittered by many regrets; and it is by the feelings you purpose to indulge that I have blotted out their remembrance."

" In mercy such comforts are sent to make life endurable," replied Emmeline. " The harp of sorrow shall hang upon the walls to moulder in the dust, and pour forth a joyful note of gladness that will come deep from my breast."

" It gives me joy to hear you," said the fair hostess ; " but we must prepare for the coming banquet ; my Lord only returned yesternight, and the whole Castle are to be assembled at the board to greet him."

" I shall only be too ready to add my congratulations," said Emmeline ; " and heartily do I rejoice that heaven, in smiling mercy, has restored your good lord to this home. Nor shall I forget to invoke a blessing on this domain, whenever I lay my head on the pillow of slumber."

" I believe you, in all sincerity," answered the Lady of Arundel ; " and, while life shall last, whether in scenes of trouble or joy, in all my dreams of hope, in sickness, or in health, I'll think of thee."

The two ladies are now seated at the massive oak table which surrounded the olden hall. It groaned under the load of good cheer. At the upper end of the apartment was a raised dais, where the noble Lord of the Castle entertained his distinguished guests. A whole side of venison was placed before him on a huge salver, and there, seated behind the lordly dish, he received the congratulations of his retainers, and witnessed the numerous pastimes that followed. Various rude dances were executed, in which little Kitty excelled brilliantly; and, as the zeal of the performers flagged with the excess of exertion, several songs and lighter amusements passed the hours gaily away.

On these occasions the fame of King Alfred was never forgotten, the founder of the domain being always regarded with feelings almost amounting to veneration. At a suitable pause, seized by a momentary train of inspiration, the fair hostess did justice to that renowned mon-arch in verse that perhaps might have provoked a smile from a modern poet laureate. Her song declaimed that the fame of the great King should last when the surrounding walls had crumbled to decay. She told how he led his valiant followers against the mighty Danes. How his name was blessed by loving friends who sighed in oppres-sion. How he shed music forth while foes stood listening around. She declared how he gave not only learning, but both laws and arts to his countrymen, and taught the poor and lowly slave. Then, in sweet and plaintive notes, she implored for peace to his immortal soul. Her song was listened to with marked reverence by a numerous audience.

When these amusements were concluded, amid a burst of approbation, Lady Emmeline was requested to prolong the diversion with an exhibition of her skill. Considering the excitement recently endured, she might easily have excused herself, but unwilling to mar the pleasure of this joyful occasion, she did her best, and, somewhat nervously, warbled rather than sung the following simple ditty :—

" Quiet, through the calmness of the stilly night,
Peaceful in dreaming slumber I recline,
Ah ! why did fate my dearest joys so blight,
And leave me long in solitude to pine ?

But hope sustained my sad and weary days,
The hours of gloom for ever cannot last.
With joy, I soon will sing my cheerful lays,
Forgetting all the care and sorrow past."

It was a late hour before the guests retired to prepare for the continuance of their journey on the morrow, the amusements still proceeding with great spirit. But one fair maiden never closed her eyes to sleep. She thought of the morrow, when once more the old walls of Pevensel would give her rest. She thought of meeting her uncle so changed, and so sensible of fatal errors in the years that had passed. And as she looked upon the bright stars that beamed through the open lattice, she poured forth to heaven a lofty song, and listening, as the western breeze carried their sounds away, she wished the notes could be wafted far to the olden walls, which she soon hoped to enter in triumph, with one so lately forbidden their shelter.

Morn again rose in brilliant splendour, and the travellers took leave of their hospitable host and hostess. The men-at-arms lined their way for a considerable distance in single file, the lord himself accompanying them for two or three miles. The two noble ladies parted at the gate—"Farewell —but, remember, that though parted, hearts may be not less true." It was an exchange of good-will, and fondest hope. Oppression's arm was no longer strong. Those mutual sorrows, those

sudden joys had built the firm structure of
friendship, to endure until the end of life itself.
The noble lady is again watching on a lofty
tower, until the wayfarers are lost in the distant
view.

But a new surprise now awaited them. They
are on the summit of those lofty downs that
overlook the domains of Pevensel. The proud
towers are distinctly visible, but no banner floats
above them. Where, then, is the noble lord?
Time will shew. Though, with beating heart,
Emmeline passed the outer gate of the fortress.
The servants stare in blank bewilderment, the
master had not arrived, and it was in anxious
conjecture that the night passed away. On the
following day, about noon, two figures are seen
on the watch tower. One, a bold Knight,
watches the distant hills, while a tender maiden
hung closely on his shoulder. Often she had

looked from that tower in dreamy sadness, long-ing for one that she loved. That one was now by her side. But again she scanned the barren downs with an overflowing soul. Nor does she look in vain. A proud cavalcade wends its way over those mossy heights, and gave a lustre to the scene, already impressive in the grandeur of nature.

It was once more the old home of childhood. Lady, with your presence, awake the faded glories of its cheerfulness. Many bright suns will fall upon its towers, but your smiles can shed a deeper lustre within. Go down, now, and meet the guardian of your youth ; he is feeble and aged. He has but one object in life, your future happiness his only thought. His trembling steps advance, his fond embrace is ready to receive that tender form. He comes—the weep-ing girl stands clasped in his arms ! These are tears of joy; tears that speak the inward passion of the soul for want of utterance, as he placed her fair hand in the palm of a noble youth who stood close by. The aged lips invoke the blessing of heaven upon a happy union, and in a manly openness, the noble lord declared the moment come he had so long dreaded, and it was the happiest in his life.

It is necessary to account for the delay. The enfeebled state of the noble lord rendered many halts imperative on the return from Guildford. He was a weary pilgrim fast journeying to the shrine of eternal rest. His eye had lately been dimmed by many a sorrow, and, though the evening of life had come, yet there was peace for his remaining days. That confidence between him and the lovely maiden, so long broken, was fully restored in all its early purity. In his hours of pleasure, in the time of sickness, or under the heavy load of trouble that infirmity must entail, there was that tender girl hovering round his path, like an angel in the form of humanity.

But there was another crown of happiness, wherein she was to shine as the brightest jewel. One is near who had never loosened his rivetted and raptured gaze from her beauteous face ! Oh, holy angels, is there no paradise on earth ? There is ! it is simply for the brighter attributes of our nature to seek it out. There is a noble youth present who has found it. He had followed the path of duty; he fought in many a good cause a battle of desperation, but he found at last the regions of peace. It was in the holy simpleness of that lovely girl. It was not a poor and mortal sentiment, it hinged on the heavenly and the divine !

CHAPTER XIII.

> " Not for themselves alone
> Our fathers lived ; nor with a niggard hand
> Raised they the fabrics of enduring stone,
> Which yet adorn the land ;
> Their piles, vast monuments of the mighty dead,
> Survive them still, majestic in decay ;
> But ours are like ourselves, I said,
> The creatures of a day."
>
> SOUTHEY.

AFTER a brief stay at Pevensel, Sandford again engaged in the service of the Prince. A few rebels, who still held out against the King's authority, had to be reduced to submission ; and on the Palm Sunday in the year subsequent to the events just detailed, the Prince attacked the old town of Winchelsea, and inflicted a severe chastisement for their piratical and lawless acts. A few days after the Easter that immediately followed, the marriage of our hero with the Lady Emmeline was celebrated with great pomp. A number of distinguished knights honoured the ceremony with their presence, and attired in rich silk cointoins, they added to the brilliancy of this joyful occasion.

The first two years of their married life was mostly spent in the old home. At the expiration of that time, the noble lord succumbed to the iron hand of death. His end was peace, he lived a sufficient time for all recollections of the past to wear away; and that devoted girl who was the charm of his life, closed his eyes at the last. This event prevented Sandford and Emmeline's presence at the marriage of Conisburgh

and little Kitty, which was celebrated at Winchelsea the day before Savoy departed this life.
It was necessary to wait the return of her uncle
from Spain. The mystery of her mother was
only discovered shortly after Sandford became a
husband; its first effect was to damp the little
maiden's spirits for a short time, but they soon
recovered their former buoyancy.

While Morton remained at Hurstingham,
Conisburgh went to France to seek the treasure
left by Margot, and at the attack on Winchelsea
several valuables belonging to the murdered
seaman were recovered. The proceeds rendered
their possessor a man of independence, though he
remained in Sandford's service.

After Savoy's death the Castle at Pevensel
passed to the Crown, and Sandford took up his
residence permanently at Hurstingham. Here
many years were passed in one unceasing devo-

tion to his beloved spouse, but he was still engaged in the Prince's service, and when that noble warrior ascended the throne, he still accompanied him in several bloody wars, and at an advanced age fell nobly in the cause of the master he had so ardently served.

His whole career was one of honourable exertion, nor did its fruit pass away with the end of his life. His name was long remembered by a grateful monarch, and cherished by all his servants. In him the weak and oppressed found a constant friend. When the cold damp of death was on his cheek, and his voice faltered in faint and inaudible tones, he did not forget that all his energies had been aroused to one unceasing discharge of duty, both to his country and his home. And so he fought the great battle of life, a conflict that presented one continued scene of brilliant victory, the result of perseverance, of genius, and of courage.

As she had lived in girlhood, so the Lady Emmeline passed through life. There was the same simplicity of nature, though strengthened by experience. The days of mourning for her uncle over, she dwelt mostly in seclusion at Hurstingham. Considerate for the affections of all her menials, she also administered to the wants of those who had need of this world's goods, and so her days passed away in the fulfilment of every duty that becomes a loving wife, and a joyful mother of children. Then as a widow, it was not in a momentary tear that she mourned the loss of an adored husband, but in a holy contemplation of his joys, as greater than this earth could afford, even under the influence of her winning smiles. Attended to the last by the faithful Anne, who became the wife of one of Sandford's principal officers, she reached the seventh stage of human existence, and vanished peacefully into eternity.

* * * *

Such is the conclusion of our story. Six centuries have rolled away, and the ferocity of a lawless age has softened before an era of advanced civilization. After sustaining another siege, in which it was bravely defended by the Lady Pelham, and after serving as a prison house for the Duke of York, in the reign of Henry IV., and also for Joan of Navarre, the spouse of that same monarch, who, with her father confessor, the Prior Randal, was accused of a design to destroy the King, still to future times, the broken ruin of noble Pevensey remains a decaying monument of former pride, and almost forgotten grandeur. Forsaken by the mighty sea, which once nearly washed the base of its now fallen towers, an object of curiosity's gaze, the haunt of the night owl, those ivy-mantled walls slowly crumble into dust, while the tide of human events rolls onward through its varied course;

until the end of all things transient is attained, as a tale is brought to its CONCLUSION.

"The mouldering marble lasts its day,
Yet falls at length a useless fane,
To ruin's ruthless fangs a prey,
The wrecks of pillar'd pride remain."

BYRON.

THE END.

T. C. NEWBY, 30, Welbeck Street, Cavendish Square, London.